DISCOVERED TRANSGRESSIONS

DISCOVERED TRANSGRESSIONS

JULIE BAWDEN DAVIS

Roses
ARE
RED
PUBLISHING

ISBN 13: 978-1-955265-35-5

ISBN 10: 1-955265-35-6

Distributed by Roses Are Red Publishing

rosesareredpublishing.com

 Created with Vellum

ACKNOWLEDGMENTS

As they say, it takes a village. Here's my village. I'm supremely grateful to each of these fabulous people!

ARC Reading Gems

Julie Schlueter

Tara Bradley

Susa Fraccaroli

Kery Bailey

Trish Darrenkamp

Marilyn Smith

Lisa Starkey

Heather Wamboldt

Beth Helm

Teresa Reitnauer

Chelle Young

Asra Syed

Tanya Wheeler

Jacquelyn Gray

Penny McCulloch

Amber Mancebo

Pros

Sharon Whatley, editing

Judy Bullard, cover design

Kyle Kane, logo design

Sabrina Wildermuth, design consultation

Jeremy Davis, technical support

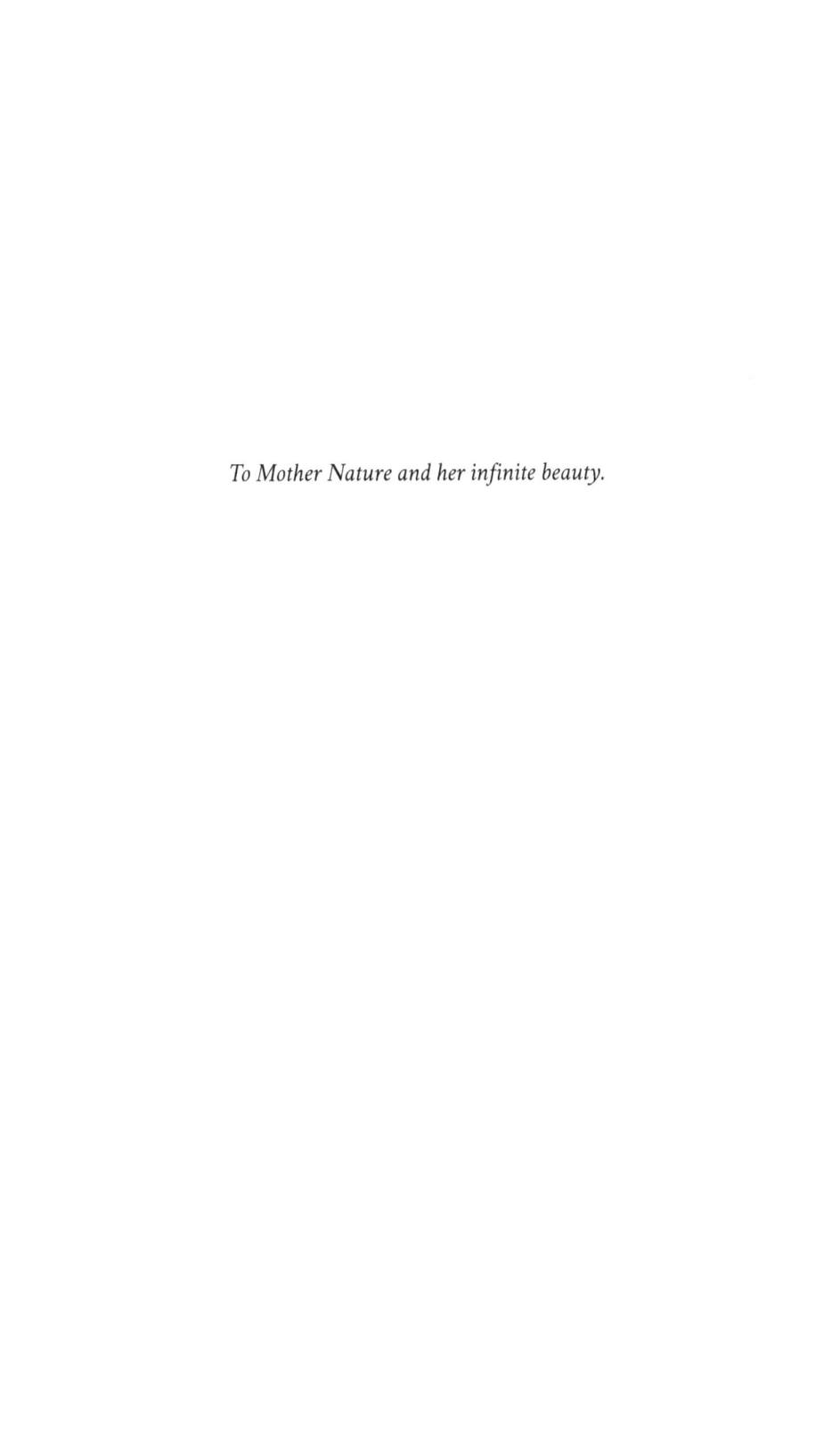

To Mother Nature and her infinite beauty.

"You can't catch me, Aunt Savannah Banana!"

"You get over here, you little rascal." Savannah grabbed a dry noodle from the package of spaghetti and held it aloft as she chased her nephew across the kitchen and down the hall. Giggling as he ran, Flynn flew into the bathroom and slammed the door shut, locking it.

Savannah tapped on the door. "Open up, or I'll pick the lock."

"No fair!" She heard the five-year-old's breathing coming quick on the other side of the door. A warm feeling melted through her at the affection she felt for the little boy.

"What do you mean, no fair?" she asked.

"I can't pick locks like you can."

"Open up, and I'll teach you how."

She could practically hear her nephew thinking on the other side of the door.

Just then Savannah's sister called out, "I'm back!"

Flynn flung open the bathroom door as Jolene entered the hallway.

"What are you two up to?" Jolene looked from Flynn to

Savannah. It had started to drizzle outside, and her sister's black hair glistened with moisture.

"Aunt Banana is going to teach me how to pick a lock." Flynn smiled, his brown eyes flashing with excitement.

"We were just playing around." Savannah looked down at the noodle in her hand and remembered the water boiling on the stove. "I've got to put the spaghetti in," she said, scooting past her sister.

Back in the kitchen, Savannah mixed in the spaghetti with a wooden spoon as her cell phone pinged. She reached over and checked the text. *I finished the blood tests you wanted done. There's something I think you're going to want to see. I can stick around if you want me to.*

Savannah sighed and stirred, her stomach rumbling at the scent of the simmering red sauce she'd made.

"You don't look happy," said Jolene, walking into the kitchen. Her sister had pulled her hair into a ponytail and changed out of her dress into jeans and a T-shirt. Jolene didn't look much different than when they were teenagers, Savannah thought, with slim, almost straight hips, and good skin that quickly blushed red when she was embarrassed. Growing up, people often commented the two of them were true southern belles, one dark haired, the other blonde.

Jolene took the spoon from Savannah's hand. "Is it work? I thought you were done for the day."

Savannah stepped back from the simmering pot and glanced at her phone again. "I thought I was, too, but my lab tech found something that could be of importance to the case we're working on. As usual, time is of the essence."

"You can go. The sauce smells delicious, by the way. Mark is going to love it."

Savannah groaned. "I'm salivating and starving." She grabbed a spoon and dipped it into the sauce and took a taste, then tapped into her phone and went to get her purse off the kitchen table. After slipping into her heels, she put on her holster and took her gun off the top of the refrigerator, sliding the weapon in and pulling on her jacket.

"Sorry about the lock picking. I forget sometimes he's only five," said Savannah.

Jolene added a dollop of oil to the boiling noodles. "He forgets, too. I told him he'd have to wait until he was eighteen to learn that useful skill. He's pouting in his room now."

"Tell him I'll teach him how to tuck and roll, instead," said Savannah, laughing as she headed out of the kitchen and into the wet March evening.

After sitting in gridlock on the Arlington Memorial Bridge over the Potomac, Savannah pulled into FBI headquarters and parked in the garage. She wondered what the new development might be. They had been combing over evidence from a home invasion for days and hadn't uncovered anything.

When she entered the lab, she found her tech peering into a microscope at the counter. "I thought you were going to go home?" Savannah asked as she approached.

Cherie Tomlinson slid her perfect size-four frame off the stool, glittering blue sneakers hitting the floor. "I found something in one of the blood samples." Her red bob bounced as she talked, and her eyes lit up.

Savannah stepped forward and peered through the lens, studying the cell structure for a moment. "Whoever belongs to this blood has Huntington's Disease," she murmured.

"None of the victims show signs of the condition," said the lab tech.

"This is great work," said Savannah. "Any word from DNA on the blood?"

Savannah grinned at the young woman's habit of knitting her brow when all the pieces of a case hadn't yet come together. "Not yet. Hopefully by morning."

"Go home and get some sleep," said Savannah. "You need a ride?"

"No, the subway is still running," said Cherie, hanging her backpack from one shoulder as she glanced out the window. "And it looks like the rain stopped."

Savannah nodded; glad they finally had a solid lead. The director of her unit was expecting a suspect sooner than later. It looked like she might be able to fulfill that order soon.

Minutes later, Savannah's heels echoed in the FBI headquarters' parking garage. She pushed the keypad on the side of her car, then got in and took off her jacket and holster and gun, setting everything on the seat next to her. Keys in the ignition, she was about to turn on the engine when someone opened the back door and slid into the seat behind her. In the rearview mirror, she saw a person wearing a black ski mask and wielding a gun.

"Eyes forward, and keep your hands on the steering wheel," said a man's voice.

Savannah tightened her hands on the wheel and glanced out of the corner of her eye at her gun. Her visitor would get a shot off before she even had a chance to reach for it.

"I won't hurt you," said the voice behind the mask. "I just want you to listen."

"What do you want?" asked Savannah, chest tight with anxiety.

"Justice," said the voice. The person handed her a manila envelope over her right shoulder.

"What's in here?"

"Something you need to see."

"If this contains ricin, I'm going to make sure you get a good dose, too," warned Savannah.

"This is a different kind of deadly," said the voice. "Open the envelope."

Savannah lifted the clasp and pulled up on the flap, then reached in and removed some photographs.

"Is this a joke?" she asked, flipping through the photos, a series of strikingly exotic orchids.

"No," her assailant's voice became agitated. "Unless you call millions of dollars of contraband a joke."

"I don't think I've ever seen this species of orchids before. Are they rare?"

"The rarest, Agent Sanchez."

"You obviously know who I am. You should also know the FBI doesn't have jurisdiction over plants. If someone is stealing endangered orchids, you need to call Fish and Wildlife."

"The FBI does have jurisdiction over murder."

"You're telling me someone was killed over these orchids?"

"More than someone. There's a contact name in the envelope. He can tell you more."

Savannah opened the envelope again and spotted a card at the bottom. She reached in to retrieve it when her captor jumped out of the car. Tossing the envelope and picking up her gun, she opened her car door and yelled, "Stop!" But her mystery visitor had disappeared.

2

Savannah studied the business card left by her unknown visitor. It read Brent Larson, Chief Arborist, National Forest Association. She turned the card over to see a phone number scribbled on the back. Tapping the card against the steering wheel, she wondered what kind of game was being played here. Then she picked up one of the orchid photos and turned on her car light and studied it. She knew about orchids, since her mother and grandmother ran a nursery back in Georgia. The foliage was distinctly serrated. Very unusual for a *dendrobium*, if that's what she was looking at.

Her stomach rumbled again, reminding her she never ate. She glanced at the clock. Nearly nine pm. Too late to go back to Jolene's. Putting the car in reverse, she backed out of her parking space and headed for home, glancing at the photos on the passenger seat as she drove.

When she opened the door to her two-bedroom apartment, her heart hitched like it often did when she stepped into the stillness. It had been five years since Jaime's passing, but sometimes she still got a lump in her throat when she came home to a quiet house. In the bedroom, she took off her heels, jacket, and holster, then went into the kitchen and pulled a bottle of pinot out of the fridge. After pouring herself a glass, she took a sip, then grabbed a jar of mixed nuts from the cupboard and went to the living room. She sat down on the couch, where she often dozed off at night, and turned on the television, grateful for how the sound filled the empty apartment.

Brent Larson awoke in the early morning, disoriented, until he remembered where he was. He glanced around his old room as his eyes focused in the still dim light. This trip home to Poolesville had been long overdue. Time to clear out the family home and decide if he and his sister were going to sell. It was something he'd had a hard time addressing, because then he'd have to say goodbye to so many good memories. True, he wasn't planning on moving back here anytime soon, but with the house still theirs, the memories were always accessible here in his childhood home.

Hoisting himself out of bed, he pulled on sweats and a long-sleeved shirt, then walked over the creaky wooden floor and downstairs to the farm-style kitchen. He pulled the chicory root bag out of the cupboard and measured some granules into the coffeemaker. As it percolated, the brew's sweet, smoky scent filling the kitchen, he glanced out the back window at the giant white oak his grandmother had planted fifty years ago. Shrugging on his down jacket, he stepped out the back door into the crisp, early morning. When he got to the tree, a nuthatch flew from one of the limbs and landed in a nearby hedge of holly. It began madly pecking at the deep-red berries. Brent knew his chicory was likely done, but if he moved, the bird would fly away and abandon her feast. He stayed stock still, watching as the nuthatch filled its belly. When she finished and flew off, he returned to the kitchen. Time for what he came back to Maryland for: sorting through his parents' things.

"Brent! Mom wants you to help out with dinner." At his younger sister's shouting, the mourning dove Brent had been observing for the past twenty minutes flew off, his wings making the distinctive creaking sound as the bird headed into the forest surrounding their property. Fifteen at the time, Brent felt the familiar frustration of having such a bossy, intrusive sister. He loved Becky, but she always interrupted him. He sat back on his haunches and wrote in his notebook about the bird's behavior when his ten-year-old sister arrived by his side, panting. "There you are! Mom's been calling your name for half an hour."

Brent held up a finger to silence her for a moment as he finished his last bit of description: long, thin tail, black dots on its wings. Then he slapped his notebook shut and stood, his lanky body dwarfing his sister's short stature. "I heard you the first time, and so did the bird I was observing. He flew away."

Becky cocked her head at Brent, a scowl on her face. "The birds should know by now you're not going to hurt them. You watch them all the time. Why don't they learn like Ramrod?"

"Dogs are different than birds, like I've explained before," he said as they walked toward the house together. "Why aren't you working on dinner?"

"Because I'm helping Dad oil his and mom's wheelchairs, that's why."

Brent reached over and gave his sister a gentle shove. "That's a lot better reason than last week's excuse of a jump rope contest with your friend."

Brent sat in his mother's art studio sorting through her painting supplies and filling boxes for gifting to a local artist. He looked up and admired her many landscape paintings that adorned the walls. She'd been a versatile artist and had mastered a variety of genres. But Brent's favorites had always been the outdoor scenes. Most were of the terrain surrounding their home, but some were of Norway, where his grandparents were from. His eye went to a particular piece she had hanging on the opposite wall that had enthralled him since he was a young boy. His mother called it Night Lights. The sky was dark, except for a moon rising and a sky studded with stars that appeared to twinkle. Though she had bequeathed many of her paintings to an art gallery in DC, she had left Brent and his sister some of her work, and Night Lights was his. He knew exactly where he'd hang it back home in North Carolina.

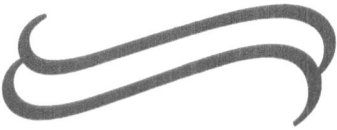

Savannah called the lab the next morning and asked Cherie to check out Brent Larson. Then she jumped on her elliptical machine for thirty minutes before showering and heading into the office.

An hour later, she walked into the fingerprinting lab at headquarters, where she found Robbie sealing a baseball bat into an evidence bag. He gently set down the bat and pushed up his wire-rimmed glasses with gloved hands. "Boss, what's up?"

"Was that for the home invasion case?"

"Yeah, no prints, unfortunately."

Savannah handed him the orchid envelope. "Hopefully you'll have better luck with this. I compromised them, but I'm hoping you'll find someone else's prints, as well."

Robbie peered into the envelope. "Sure. When you need it?"

"Now would be nice."

He glanced at the clock on the wall. "You going to wait?"

Savannah nodded and took a seat on a nearby stool. She watched as he removed the photos and the business card, laying them out on a clear space on the countertop. He took out a new fingerprinting brush and dipped it lightly into powder, then expertly twirled the brush over the photos.

"The nice thing about photos is the glossy finish," he said, almost to himself. "Prints tend to show up pretty good. There. I've got a really good one. Probably not yours, because the print looks large." He took a photo, then entered it into IAFIS, the FBI's fingerprint identification system, which began searching.

"Is this a case you're working on?" he asked.

"Just something I'm checking out," said Savannah.

Robbie grabbed a coffee mug that said lab rat on the side and took a quick swig. Just then, the machine dinged, indicating they had a match. He checked the screen and frowned. "Odd."

Savannah got off the stool to stand beside him. "Why's that?"

"The owner of the fingerprint died during an FBI raid of a counterfeiting operation six months ago."

3

Savannah stared at the face of an older man, his eyes hard, his expression grim.

"A long rap sheet," said Robbie, giving a low whistle.

She nodded in agreement as she read his history. Forgery, smuggling stolen goods, counterfeiting. "A one-man shop." She tapped her foot on the floor as she tried to make sense of this. "How'd he die?"

Robbie touched the computer screen. "In crossfire during the sweep. Gunshot wound to the neck." He peered closer at the screen. "Will known associates help you?"

"Sure, email me everything. I have to check in with Cherie. She's working on some blood analysis, and we're waiting on DNA."

As Savannah made her way through the halls, she thought about her unknown visitor. He must have worn gloves the entire time he handled the photos. Her phone lit up with an email from Robbie that she opened while she walked. The first name on the list of associates she recognized immediately. Clyde Cooper. She and the team had put him away a couple of years ago for running a massive forgery ring. Now that Cooper was potentially involved, this orchid thing suddenly looked a lot more serious.

When Brent's phone lit up, he saw it was Becky calling. He set down the handful of brushes in his hand and answered.

"What time do I pick you up at Dulles?" he asked.

"About that."

Brent stared up at the ceiling. "What did Russ do this time?"

"Nothing. It's good news, actually."

"Go on."

"Remember that hair commercial part? I got it. Can you believe it?"

Visions of his sister's long, flowing auburn hair flashed across Brent's mind. "Yes, I can believe it. That's great news."

"They start filming tomorrow at a studio in downtown LA."

Brent glanced around his mom's room and at the empty boxes lined up against the wall.

"Are you mad at me?" his sister asked.

"No. Irritated, maybe, since you're the one pushing to sell the place. But I'll be fine. You know I prefer the quiet anyway."

His sister giggled. "You mean you prefer not to hear my constant babbling." She paused. "About selling. If it's too soon, we can hold off. Mrs. Sullivan said she's happy to keep an eye on things as long as we need."

"How about this? You shoot your commercial and get

famous, then we'll reconvene. Go memorize your lines or whatever it is you do."

"I'll probably just be swinging my hair around."

Brent laughed. "You've been doing that since we were kids."

His sister was quiet for a moment. "You okay?" she asked him, her voice lowering. "You and mom were so close."

"I'll be fine," Brent said, picking up a paintbrush and examining the tip, still tinged with green paint.

"Call me anytime if you need to talk. And go out and do something fun. Is that girl Karen still around? Call her."

"I doubt her husband would appreciate that."

"You're hopeless." His sister sighed.

"Stop worrying about my love life and focus on your own. I gotta go."

"Love you."

"Love you exponentially more."

"Any word on the DNA?" Savannah asked Cherie when she arrived in the lab.

Cherie was working on a laptop set up on the counter. "Not yet. But I did dig up some info on Brent Larson. He looks clean. Although I'm not sure what you're looking for." The lab tech looked at Savannah expectantly. "He's nice looking. Where'd you meet him?"

"I haven't."

"Oh, a case then?"

"Maybe," said Savannah, explaining what happened with the masked man.

"Wow. Now you have to find this Brent guy." Cherie grinned. "No mention of a spouse, by the way."

Savannah groaned inwardly, hoping Cherie wasn't going to bug her to join the dating scene, but her assistant was sidetracked by a call on the lab's phone and sprang up to get it.

While Cherie talked, Savannah took the opportunity to check out Larson's information. As his card indicated, he was a certified arborist. In addition to his position with the Forest Foundation, he worked for the US Forest Service in North Carolina. His record was spotless. Not even a parking ticket. He had a younger sister who lived in Los Angeles, and his parents were deceased. His mom had passed away less than a year ago. She looked over at Cherie, still talking on the phone, then snuck another glance at Larson. He was handsome with his square jaw and bright blue eyes that looked straight into the camera.

"Good news," said Cherie, hanging up. "We got a match from DNA. And the blood sample is positive for Huntington's."

"Who's the match to?"

"The father-in-law. He hasn't been into work for two days, and he made a reservation on a flight to Rio de Janeiro this morning. It leaves Dulles in two hours."

"He's on the run," said Savannah as she rushed out of the lab.

Outside the studio window, Brent saw the day bright and clear. It'd be nice to take a break. He finished filling a box with art supplies and went to put it by the door when his phone rang. He pulled it out of his jeans pocket and checked the screen. It was Abdul, his colleague who headed up the National Wildlife Federation's Crimes Against Nature Taskforce.

"Abdul, what's up?"

"They took them," the man cried.

"Took what?"

"The orchids we hadn't yet identified. On the north shore."

"Are you sure? Those orchids are like gold."

"I have photos. The area has been picked clean!"

"Okay, try to remain calm. I thought you took some specimens."

"I did. They're in the station and fortunately still alive. But the ones growing in the wild are gone. I thought you were going to do something about this?"

Brent ran a hand through his hair. "I've been trying to track down the poachers, but we're understaffed, especially since Bruce died."

Abdul was silent for a moment. "My apologies. I know you are doing your best. Especially after Mr. Patterson died so suddenly."

"It's your job to protect endangered plants, Abdul. And you do it well. I'll talk to you in a few days when I'm back in town. We'll figure out how to handle this."

As Brent hung up the phone, his mind flashed to Bruce, and a feeling of unease overtook him. The doctor had ruled his colleague's death a heart attack, but Brent knew how active the man had been and how rigorously he watched his diet. Given this recent news about the poachers becoming even more brazen, Brent wondered, could Bruce's death be somehow connected?

4

After catching the assailant at the airport with her team, he caved within fifteen minutes of questioning and confessed to everything. Savannah checked her watch. Almost noon. If she hit the road now, she'd make it to the super max prison in Maryland by three for a visit with Cooper.

Once in the car headed toward Cumberland, she ran through the Cooper case. Two years ago, he'd been running his forgery ring out of a warehouse in Baltimore. What landed him in a super max prison was the extent of his operation, which reached across the globe and raked in multi-millions every year.

At the North Branch Correctional Institution, Savannah headed up the sidewalk to the expansive, block-style brick building. She'd called ahead during her drive, and they were expecting her. As she handed over her firearm at the front desk, she took a deep breath. Though she'd been to numerous prisons over the course of her decade-long career, she still got the willies knowing the crimes many of the prisoners had committed. She looked straight ahead as she followed the prison guard to cell block four, ignoring the catcalls and sound of bars rattling. She had asked for a room, and Cooper was already inside it, sitting handcuffed to a table.

"You want me to go in with you?" the guard asked.

She shook her head. "I'll let you know if I need you." As he opened the heavy metal door and she walked in and it banged closed behind her, an icy feeling slipped down her spine.

Cooper had his bald head lowered, his eyes staring at his handcuffed fists. She went to the opposite side of the table and pulled out the metal chair, the sound of its legs scraping along the concrete floor echoing in the small room.

A few beats after she sat down, Cooper lifted his head, his dark, glasslike stare hostile. "If it isn't the infamous Agent Sanchez." He puckered his mouth with disdain and looked away.

"It's been a while, Cooper," she said.

"You were never good at small talk," he growled. "What do you want?"

"Some information." She set the envelope of orchid photos on the table between them.

He turned and eyed the envelope, then leaned back in his chair and scrutinized her face. "You getting sleep, Sanchez? I hear you're sleeping alone nowadays."

Savannah kept her face immobile at the dig about Jaime. "You were never good at small talk either, Cooper." She made a point of glancing at the watch on her arm.

Sensing he might soon lose his audience, Cooper looked up at the ceiling, then leaned toward her across the table. "What do you have in your mystery envelope, and what's in it for me?"

"Give me something useful, I'll see about getting you extra privileges."

He considered a moment, then lifted his shackled hands. "You're going to have to open it yourself."

Savannah reached into the envelope and pulled out the photos, spreading them in front of Cooper.

He eyed the orchids, then laughed. "You taking up gardening, Sanchez?"

Savannah watched his face closely and saw the telltale muscle near his right eye move. She knew that well from the hours she'd spent interrogating him about his operation.

"Your superintendent tells me you complain about the food here. I'll get something a lot tastier to you—pizza, burnt prime ends, maybe your favorite cherry danish. I'll keep it coming, depending on how well your info serves me."

Cooper grinned at her and shifted in his seat. Savannah knew he was already salivating.

"I can tell you know something about these photos," Savannah said, unblinking.

Cooper looked away, then back at her and shrugged. "What the hell. I'm suddenly feeling generous." He hesitated for several moments, the silence between them suspended. "You're looking for William Macintosh."

The name hit Savannah in the gut, but she kept her voice even. "Macintosh died five years ago in an explosion."

Cooper met her gaze. "He escaped the explosion, and he's alive and into black market plants—orchids, in particular." Cooper gestured to the photos with his chin. "Trust me, he's found a way to get his hands on something this rare."

"How do you know he's still alive?"

"I want a guaranteed delivery every week."

Savannah tapped her heel quietly on the concrete floor as she studied his face. She had seen Macintosh shot, and the building blast afterward, but Cooper seemed to be telling the truth.

"Where can I find him?"

"That I don't know, but I can tell you he's been delivering his plants to Japanese collectors in and out of the country."

Savannah leaned back in the chair and put her arms across her chest. "Where is he getting the orchids from?"

"Throw in some tequila."

Savannah knew he was on the hook. "Rest assured. It's as good as under your mattress."

"Croatian National Forest in North Carolina."

On her way back to DC, Savannah dialed the cell phone number in Larson's file. She got his voicemail. "Mr. Larson, my name is Savannah Sanchez. I'm calling about something that has come to my attention regarding orchids. Can you call me back at this number at your earliest convenience? Thank you." Generally, Savannah would have identified herself as FBI, but this didn't feel like official business yet. She turned up the music for the ride home.

Brent walked around the property obsessing over the stolen orchids. Abdul had good reason to be upset. The climate in that part of North Carolina was like few places in the world, so there was a good chance the specimens were the only ones. The fact that poachers had removed them all was a horticultural travesty. Thankfully, Abdul had the fore-sight to take some cuttings and had propagated samples, so at least they weren't completely lost. He thought about the poachers. A person needed to be an expert, like Abdul, to ensure that plants taken from their native habitat survived. That meant keeping them in the correct temperature and ensuring the proper humidity levels.

He stopped and looked around the property. There was a lot to do here in Poolesville, but he really needed to get back home soon and protect the remaining field of rare orchids. It was just a matter of time before they were also compromised. He thought again about Bruce and the day before he died, stopping short in his tracks when he realized that his colleague had been out to the orchid field that day. Bruce had even texted Brent to call him when he got a chance, but Brent never got the opportunity before his colleague died. Now he wondered, what had Bruce wanted to tell him?

5

When Brent returned to the house, he took off his coat and went to the kitchen island to check his phone. A voicemail from a woman with a southern accent. When she mentioned orchids, he pulled out a stool and sat down. She had called just twenty minutes ago. He dialed her number, but the call went to voicemail.

"This is Agent Savannah Sanchez with the Federal Bureau of Investigation. If this is an emergency, please hang up and dial 911. Otherwise, leave a message after the beep. And have a great day."

The mention of the FBI gave Brent pause. He debated hanging up, but after a couple seconds decided to leave a message. "This is Brent Larson. I'm returning your call, Agent Sanchez. You've got my number." Then he hung up and stared at the kitchen island his mother had inlaid with blue and white ceramic tile. The FBI was involved with this?

He glanced at the clock and realized he hadn't eaten in hours. Yanking open the freezer, he dug around until he found a casserole dish encased in a plastic freezer bag. Written in his mom's meticulous hand, the label read: *Meat-*

balls and Ziti. The date was just two weeks before her passing. He slid the dish out and held it for a moment, envisioning her in the kitchen, then put it in the microwave on defrost. It'd be nice to have one of his mom's home-cooked meals right about now.

"What's it like having two parents who are crippled? How'd that happen, anyway?" asked Brent's senior prom date, Tracy. They were outside of the high school in the smoking area with some other kids, sneaking a few beers. Her comment shut everyone up, and they all turned to Brent. She had asked the question many people were too uncomfortable to ask.

"It's disabled. And it's fine," said Brent. "Just like other parents."

Tracy took a slug of beer. "How would you know that it's like other parents? Were they normal once?"

Brent stood up straighter and took a deep breath. "Just because their legs don't work doesn't mean they're not normal. My mother was born with a birth defect and has always been in a wheelchair, and my dad lost the use of his legs when he was a teenager. They met at school."

Tracy looked thoughtful for a moment. "So, they're high school sweethearts?"

Brent spooned a generous portion of pasta onto an earthenware plate, then brought it over to the wooden table his dad had made. He was getting himself a fork when his phone rang. He reached for it on the kitchen island and checked the screen. It was the FBI agent.

"Brent Larson."

"Mr. Larson. This is Savannah Sanchez. I'm sorry I missed your call earlier. Is this a good time?"

Brent sat back down. He smiled at the attractive accent. "Yes. Your message said you're with the FBI?"

"This isn't yet an official case. I'm just investigating at this point. I know you're based in North Carolina, but I'd like to meet, if possible."

"Actually, I'm currently in Maryland, but I'll be heading back to North Carolina in a day or two," said Brent.

"That's a stroke of luck," said the agent, her tone lightening. "I just so happen to be based in DC, so I'm not far from you. Any chance I could visit you there?"

Brent thought about Bruce and the questions beginning to form about his colleague. "That would be fine, if you could do so tomorrow." He gave her his parent's address.

Savannah hung up the phone just as she pulled up to her

31

sister's house. Through the front window, she saw her nephew and Mark, her brother-in-law, watching their big-screen TV. Her sister entered the room and went around to the back of the sofa. She leaned down to kiss them both on the top of the head. Suddenly, Savannah felt the familiar tears threaten at the back of her eyes. She remembered that feeling. Inclusiveness. That us against the rest of the world feeling. She felt the necklace she always wore around her neck, then she drove away from the house.

The next morning, Savannah made the trip to Poolesville from DC in just under an hour. When she turned onto a quiet, tree-lined street with houses set back from large front lawns, she spotted the bright-blue mailbox Larson had told her to look for. She drove down the driveway and parked in front of a low-slung, ranch-style house with smoke curling lazily from the chimney. Getting out of the car, she pulled her jacket over her emerald-green blouse and holstered gun, then headed down the front walkway lined with rosebushes, pruned to the ground and covered in hay for the winter. At the door, a bright red affair with blue flowing script across the top that read Larson, she reached for the knocker when the door swung open. In the doorway stood a muscular, light-haired man with the most intense blue eyes she'd ever seen. His expression was serious. "You must be Agent Sanchez."

Savannah pulled her identification out and showed it to him. "I am, but you can call me Savannah, Mr. Larson."

He stepped back and beckoned her to come in, saying as she passed by his tall frame, "And you can call me Brent. Let's head to the kitchen in the back. It's warmer in there."

Savannah passed through a hallway lined with family photos to the back of the house, soon entering a great room with a large, homey and comfortable kitchen, a sitting area, and a stunning view of a wooded back yard.

"Is that Sugar Loaf Mountain in the distance?" she asked, turning to him as he entered the room.

"It is. You know your way around here?" he asked, motioning for her to sit in a chair near the warm fire in the fireplace.

"One of my hobbies is studying geography. Especially maps," said Savannah.

Brent gave her a small smile and tipped his head. "That's an interesting hobby. Can I get you anything? Coffee? Water?"

"I'm fine, thank you." She glanced around the room, noting the relaxed comfort of the space. "Very nice," she said.

Brent sat across from her and smiled. "My mother was good at making things cozy." His tone changed. "She passed away a few months ago."

"I'm sorry to hear that," said Savannah.

Brent nodded, then there was an awkward moment of silence. He tapped the fingers of one hand absentmindedly on the arm of the chair he sat in, then spoke, "During your call, you said something about orchids?"

Savannah scooted to the edge of her chair and slid the orchid photos out of the envelope. "These came into my possession in an unorthodox way." She handed the photos to Brent. "Do they mean anything to you? My family owns a nursery back in Georgia, so I've seen my fair share of orchids. These look to be rare."

Brent leafed through the photos, then looked at her, his eyes wide. "I've seen these exact orchids before."

Savannah blinked, surprised. "You have?"

"Just recently, before they were poached from a boggy wildlife sanctuary in the Croatian National Forest. It's one of the areas I oversee as a forest ranger. Where did these photos come from?"

Savannah shifted in her seat, wondering how much she should tell him. "An anonymous man gave them to me and included your contact information in the envelope." She pulled out Brent's card and handed it to him. "Your cell phone number is written on the back. Do you recognize the writing?"

Brent eyed the card, then looked at Savannah with a puzzled expression. "That's my writing."

6

Brent turned the card over a few times. "I must have given this card to someone."

"Any idea who?"

She watched as his brow furrowed, recalling what Cherie had said about him. He was a very nice-looking man, even when he frowned.

Brent sighed. "I'm sorry. I do a lot of public speaking about conserving our forests, and I give my card to many people." He handed it back to her and eyed the photos. "I would love copies of those. We managed to propagate the orchids before they were poached, but pictures would be very helpful."

"I can do that," said Savannah. "You said we?"

"Abdul Farran. He oversees the Crimes Against Nature project for the American Wildlife Federation. We work together on forest preservation efforts, especially rare and native plants. He has an office at the ranger station I'm in charge of in North Carolina."

"Is there anything else you can tell me, anything at all?" asked Savannah.

Brent leaned forward slightly. "It's probably not related, but the day before my colleague Bruce Patterson died a couple of weeks ago, he said he had something to tell me. He had been in the area where the orchids were stolen that day."

Tiny alarm bells tinkled in Savannah's ears. "Your colleague died? How?"

Brent glanced at the fire, then back at Savannah. "They said it was a heart attack, but..." He stood and picked up the fire poker, then opened the grate to stoke the fire.

"But?" Savannah asked when he sat back down.

Brent looked toward the flames in the fireplace. "Bruce was one of the healthiest people I have ever known. He was only forty-five, ate well, and worked out all the time. The doctor said that spontaneous heart attacks happen sometimes, but it hasn't been sitting well with me."

Savannah eyed Brent. Her senses told her he wasn't a man who tended toward the dramatic. If he thought something was amiss, it likely was. "I think it's worth looking into your colleague's death," she said, sliding the photos back into the envelope.

Brent's eyes lit up. "So, you don't think I'm imagining things?"

Savannah stood, and Brent followed. "No, I don't. I'll likely want to talk to you more, and Mr. Farran, as well." Savannah held out her hand to shake Brent's. He had a warm, solid grasp.

Brent walked Savannah to the door and watched as she made her way to her car, her blonde hair swaying against her back. When he returned to the kitchen, he noticed a faint scent of gardenia lingering in the air. He thought about Savannah and wondered what had motivated her to pursue a career in the FBI. He spent the next few minutes wondering a lot of things about Agent Sanchez, then he forced himself to focus. He had a lot to do before leaving tomorrow.

As Savannah drove, she called the lab.

Cherie answered. "Hey boss."

"You in the middle of something?"

"Just finishing up a soil sample. What's going on?"

"Can you check into a death that occurred in North Carolina a couple of weeks ago? Name is Bruce Patterson. He is supposed to have died of a heart attack."

"You're thinking COD is wrong?"

"It's possible. The guy was only forty-five and apparently a health nut."

"I'll let you know the minute I find anything. That all you need me to do?"

"I went to visit Clyde Cooper in the super max yesterday. He claims William Macintosh is alive and in the business of stealing rare plants."

"But Macintosh is dead."

"Well, Cooper had no reason to lie. He's in for the next two decades."

"Except to screw with you," said Cherie.

"True."

"You coming in?"

Savannah glanced at the clock in her car. "In a couple of hours. I've got something to do first."

Just as Savannah hung up, her phone rang.

"How you doin', honey?" her mother asked.

"I'm fine, mama. How about you?"

"Fine and dandy. I just thought I'd check in on you."

Savannah smiled and felt the weight of the locket soft against her skin. "I appreciate that. I'm doing okay. Hey, while I've got you, could I send you some photos of orchids? They look to be rare."

"Of course. Where'd you find them?"

"I actually didn't find them. The photos were given to me. It looks like the orchids in the pictures were stolen from some US forestland in North Carolina."

"Stolen orchids are really big business," said her mother.

"I'm finding that out. I'll send the photos later tonight. Get back to me when you can."

"I will, sugar. Do something nice for yourself today."

"I will, Mama. Love to Gramma and Grampa."

"You got it."

Savannah spied a sign ahead: Forest Glades Cemetery. She pulled off and drove slowly through the open gates and headed down the road to the right. After a few minutes, she stopped the car and grabbed her jacket, then headed for the tombstone she knew well.

Brent decided to remove a dead limb on the giant oak in the yard he'd been meaning to take care of. It took him a couple of hours to saw the limb and cut it up for firewood.

He stacked it along the woodshed in the back. When he entered through the sliding glass door of the house, he heard the front door shut. Alarm bells ringing, he ran through the house and tore open the front door to see a pickup truck speeding away. Who in the hell had been in the house? He shut and locked the door, then went into the kitchen. His cell phone lay on the island where he'd left it. Maybe he had scared the intruder before they could take anything. He checked the rest of the rooms, seeing nothing out of place, until he reached the room at the end of the hall—his mother's studio. He looked at the far wall, and his stomach fell. The painting his mother gave him, the one he loved above all the others, was gone.

7

Brent searched the shelving unit that housed his mother's paintings several times, even though he knew that Night Lights wasn't there. Who would steal his mother's painting, and why? He checked the inventory list against the remaining paintings. Everything else was accounted for.

"Dammit," he muttered, grabbing his phone and doing a quick search for security companies. His sister had been wanting them to get an alarm system. He made an appointment for that afternoon. Then he called his mother's contact at the art gallery and arranged to have the bequeathed paintings picked up.

Savannah's heels sunk into the grass as she stood in front of the tombstone. "I don't have any flowers for you today. It's been busy at work," she said. A breeze picked up then, blowing her hair into her face. She pushed it back over her shoulders. "Something interesting fell into my lap. It's about plants, of all things." She looked up at the sky, emerald blue and cold, a few puffs of clouds. "Mama called and told me to do something nice for myself. She's the only one who still remembers what today is." Savannah reached down and brushed a leaf off the top of the tombstone. "Happy birthday, Jaime."

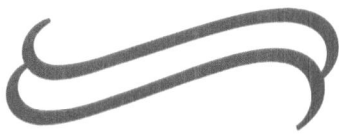

The security company talked Brent into their top system, which included remote access so he and Becky could keep an eye on the property twenty-four/seven. He asked them to put motion and broken glass sensors throughout the house, as well.

As they worked, Brent checked in with Abdul. "Any more trouble?" he asked.

"No, but I've been patrolling that area regularly."

"Good. I've been thinking we install metal baskets on top of the plants. Something to make it harder to get to them. But I'm not sure that's viable. You've been taking cuttings?"

"I have, but we need a long-term solution for this. I talked to Fish and Game."

"What'd they say?"

"That they're stretched thin and would try to come out in the next few weeks."

"I'm not sure if it amounts to anything, but a woman with the FBI is also looking into it."

"The FBI? That's great," said Abdul, his tone hopeful.

"She's particularly interested in Bruce's death, but let's keep that under wraps for now."

Abdul was silent on the other end of the line as Brent realized the gravity of what he had just said. "Be careful out there, Abdul," he added.

When Savannah returned to headquarters, she found Cherie in the lab cleaning out test tubes.

"Busy day so far?"

"Super busy," she said, setting the last one in the drainer and wiping her hands on her lab coat. "How about you?"

"Not too bad," said Savannah.

"You ever think about working with a partner again?"

Savannah eyed Cherie, wondering where this line of questioning was coming from. "I work with the team."

Cherie faced her. "I know. But you haven't partnered with anyone since Jaime."

Savannah squelched the surge of irritation she felt at the question. "I'm fine on my own. Whenever I need backup, I call for it."

Cherie glanced down at the floor, then came to meet Savannah's gaze. She opened her mouth to speak, but Savannah stopped her.

"I don't need another lecture about moving on with my life. I'll team up with someone when the right partner comes along."

"How about me?" asked Cherie.

The question surprised Savannah. "I thought you like being a lab tech?"

"I didn't want to tell you until I knew if I'd be accepted, but I'm taking the certification CSI course."

"Way to go, Cherie," said Savannah, giving her a high five. "You've come a long way from the college grad I hired five years ago."

Cherie beamed. "Thank you. I was hoping I could start going out with you sometimes to observe on crime scenes?"

"You got it," said Savannah, then paused. "I'm sorry about what I said."

"No worries." Cherie waved it away. "I know Jaime is a sensitive topic. I get it." Her expression turned thoughtful.

"You would," said Savannah softly. "Hey, your news calls for a celebration. How about a late lunch?" Just then her phone buzzed and she checked the screen. "Looks like lunch will have to wait. You ready to see your first crime scene?"

Cherie nodded her head so fast Savannah had to suppress the urge to laugh.

"Night Lights? You love that painting," said Becky. Brent had called his sister after the security system was installed.

"I talked to the local police. Maybe they'll find it. At least we took all those photos of the paintings when we were both here last."

"I think I should come home," said Becky suddenly.

"I've got it all under control, Becks. The alarm system is great. And the gallery is coming for the paintings mom donated in a little bit. Plus, Mrs. Sullivan will still be checking on the place once a day, and if something happens and the alarm company can't get ahold of us, they'll call her."

His sister sighed. "Okay, but only if you're sure."

"I'm positive. Now tell me all about your commercial. How many times did you have to swing your hair around?"

The sound of his sister laughing was just what Brent needed to hear.

Cherie impressed Savannah at the crime scene with her attention to detail and initiative. She had given her the job of combing through the shag area rug, and she had unearthed an overlooked earring. Savannah also showed her about crime scene fingerprinting when they pulled at least a dozen different prints that would show them who had been in the apartment recently. The victim, a thirty-two-year-old woman, had been stabbed and lost a lot of blood and was now unconscious at the hospital.

Savannah watched Cherie pack up her case while the coroner took over. "Great work," she told her. "How about we drop the evidence off at the lab and go for a celebratory dinner?"

Cherie smiled. "That would be great."

Savannah waited in her car while Cherie went up to the lab with the evidence. She was checking her phone for local restaurant options when the back door of the car opened. As she reached for her gun, a familiar voice warned, "Don't, Agent Sanchez. I'm here as a friend."

"Friends don't sneak into cars."

"I have new information for you." Then her visitor left just as quickly as he'd appeared and made a run for the street. She got out of the car and followed but lost him when he managed to get on the other side of a bus lumbering past. When she returned to the car, Cherie stood next to it.

"I saw you running. What happened?"

Savannah opened the door behind the driver's seat. "You have an evidence bag and gloves on you?"

Cherie unzipped her case and handed the items to Savannah, who put on the gloves and picked up a coin lying on the back seat. She held it up in the garage's dim light.

"A yen with the Phoenix rising," said Cherie. "That could be quite valuable."

Savannah slipped the coin into the bag and zipped it up. This was the second time she'd been held at gunpoint in two days. Time to get to the bottom of this.

8

Savannah slipped out of her heels and rubbed her feet together as they waited for their dinner. "I'm beat. How about you?"

Her assistant took a long drink of her iced tea and grinned. "I'm totally jazzed. I feel like I could run a marathon."

Savannah laughed. "I remember that. The first case high."

"What was your first case like?"

Savannah rubbed her fingers along the condensation on her glass. "I was fairly new to the Bureau. I'd been in the lab for a couple of years, and it was the first time I worked with Jaime. I was so nervous. I knew his reputation as a ballbuster, in terms of getting the job done at all costs. I wasn't sure I could keep up. The cops had pegged it as a home invasion, but within seconds of surveying the scene, Jaime knew it was an inside job."

Savannah stopped talking as the waitress set down a Caesar's salad in front of her. "Extra croutons and parmesan cheese," the waitress said, then turned to place a garden salad in front of Cherie. "Your burgers will be right up."

Once she had walked out of earshot, Savannah continued. "Jaime was right. The son had taken some LSD and thought his family were alien invaders."

"Oh, that's awful," said Cherie.

"It was bad, especially when the son came down and found out what he'd done. Then we went after the dealer."

They ate their salads in silence for a while. Finally, Cherie said, "Have you ever wondered what would have happened if you had remained partners? I mean, I know you couldn't once you became involved, but..." she trailed off.

"Every day of my life." Savannah sighed. "If we'd remained partners, I would have known what was going on that night, instead of what ended up happening. But then I remind myself that this is the life we sign up for as agents, and these things can and do happen. Think about that while you decide if you really want to be in the field."

Cherie nodded slowly. "I will."

Brent got off the phone with his sister and opened his laptop to catch up on emails. He scanned the recent incoming mail. Notices about forest fires in other parts of the country. Emails about the latest beetle infestations. He moved to his spam folder, deleting all the junk, until he came upon a familiar name. An email from Bruce. The subject line read: Top Secret. Brent clicked on the message, wondering if someone had spoofed Bruce's email, but once he began reading, he saw it had to be legit.

Hey Brent,

Since you couldn't talk on the phone, I thought I'd email you instead, so then we have a record of this. I was at the east end of the forest today where Abdul sighted those rare orchids. I heard voices and waited to see who it was. Two men with backpacks that I suspect had collection bags in them. They were surprised to see me. I introduced myself as the US Forest Service and told them they were on restricted land. They claimed they were lost. I'm pretty sure they were lying. I gave them directions out, but they weren't happy about it. I'm not sure how we're going to deal with this given that resources are stretched so thin, but just wanted you to know.

Bruce

His heart picking up a few beats, Brent checked the date of the email. The night before his colleague passed away. This couldn't be a coincidence. He looked at the clock. Just past eight. Not too late to call Agent Sanchez.

"Hi, Agent...Savannah," Brent said when she answered. "I just found an email in my spam from Bruce that I think is significant. Did you want me to send it to you?"

Savannah thought for a moment. "No. It'd be better for me to download onto a flash drive. Could I come by tomorrow?"

"I'm heading out early in the morning to North Carolina."

"How about I come over?" suggested Savannah. "Or would that be too much of an imposition. I could get there in about thirty minutes."

"That works. I'll see you soon." Brent hung up the phone, two thoughts on his mind. One, that this email was likely as significant as he suspected, and two, it would be nice to see Savannah again.

When the doorbell rang a little before nine, Brent shut off the show he'd been watching and went to the peephole. He saw Savannah's willowy frame standing on the steps. He ran his hands through his hair and pulled open the door.

"Thanks so much for coming out." He smiled as they stood in the entryway close to one another. Brent suddenly felt flustered. "Uh, I've got the computer in the kitchen."

Savannah followed him to the back of the house.

"Can I offer you anything?" he asked as they entered the kitchen.

"I'm fine," said Savannah. "I'll just get a copy of that email and be on my way so you can enjoy the rest of your evening."

Brent went to the island where his computer was open and gestured for her to take a look. He watched as she read the email, then tapped her shoe on the tile floor. "You wouldn't happen to have surveillance cameras out there, would you?"

Brent chuckled. "It's not unheard of in the forest, but we don't have the resources."

Savannah nodded. "Always worth checking." She took a USB drive out of her pocket and stuck it into the side of his computer. As the file downloaded, she leaned against the kitchen island, her eyes scanning the nearby window. "I see you have a security system."

Brent followed her gaze to the sensor. "I actually had the system installed this afternoon. Someone broke in earlier."

Savannah stood up from the counter. "Was anything taken?"

"A painting of my mother's."

"Your mother was an artist? Are her paintings valuable?" She looked uncomfortable at her question. "I mean, in the art world."

"They are worth quite a bit to collectors, but the interesting thing is that the person only took one painting. One she bequeathed to me."

Savannah looked thoughtful. "You call the local PD?"

"I did. But I'm not holding out much hope." He studied

her face for a moment. "You think there might be a connection between the plants and the painting?"

"I think it's something to consider." She picked up her purse to go. "You watch your back and set that alarm when I leave."

9

Savannah thought about Brent as she drove back to DC. He was a quiet sort. Of course, it could be grief, and she knew what that could do to you. From what she could gather, he seemed tight with his mother, then he also lost a colleague. She made a mental note to talk to the coroner in North Carolina first thing tomorrow morning. Brent's colleague's death was looking more and more like a murder.

Her phone rang, jolting her. It was her mother's number.

"You're calling late. What's up?"

"I don't want to alarm you, but it's your grandfather."

"Grampa? What's wrong?" Savannah noticed a truck coming up close in her rearview mirror.

"He's in the hospital. A possible stroke."

The truck neared, bearing down on Savannah as she sped up. "Is he okay?"

"For now. They've stabilized him."

Savannah reached for her gun on the passenger seat. "Can I call you right back, Mama?"

"Sure, honey, tomorrow is fine. I just wanted you to know."

Savannah threw the phone down as the truck came up beside her. She tried to get a look at the driver. A man with a baseball cap pulled low. He swerved toward her car, and she swung precariously close to the shoulder, then slowed down suddenly. As the truck lurched in front of her, she memorized the license plate number, then pulled to the side of the road, gun ready. No point in trying to outrace her pursuer. But the truck didn't stop. She waited a few minutes to put some distance between them, then started up her car and kept driving, senses on overdrive.

When the plane set down at the Coastal Carolina Regional Airport the following afternoon, Brent waited until the young family sitting next to him disembarked. Then he got up and stretched his legs and grabbed his suitcase from the overhead compartment. Once in the small terminal, he ordered an Uber to take him to the ranger station at the nearby Croatian National Forest. He noticed a text from Savannah while he'd been in the air. *Call me as soon as you can.* He dialed her number, and she picked up on the first ring.

"Brent. Where are you at?"

"I just landed in North Carolina."

"Good. I'm heading to Georgia right now. I'll be staying overnight, then coming your way tomorrow. I'll be in touch."

Brent slid his phone into the pocket of his black cords and smiled. Though he figured he'd be seeing Savannah again, he was pleasantly surprised it would be sooner than he'd thought.

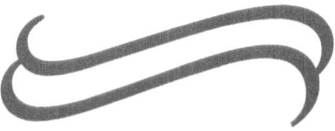

As she boarded her flight, Savannah's phone pinged. Info she had requested from Cherie on the truck that had tried to run her off the road. She took a quick look. The vehicle belonged to a Molly Stanford. No reports of it being stolen. Savannah scanned the list of known associates, her eye settling on her boyfriend's name. Jack Wallen. Priors included armed robbery. When she was seated in the airplane, she made a quick call to Cherie.

"Hey boss, you get the file I sent?"

"I did, thanks. Take a deep dive into Jack Wallen. Send me his photo. I didn't get a good look at the driver who tried to force me off the road last night, but it might jog something."

The flight attendant touched her shoulder and indicated it was time to shut off phones. Savannah nodded and powered down. She looked out the window at the Dulles tarmac scattered with patches of gray snow. It was almost as cold in Georgia. She thought about her grandparents, who had been together forty-five years. In many ways, they'd been like second parents to Savannah. She sighed and felt the locket hanging around her neck as the plane started down the runway.

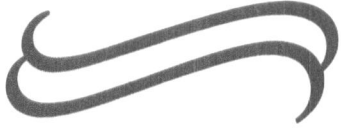

When Brent arrived at the ranger station, Abdul was

already there. He found him in the back room with the orchids. Brent cleared his throat as he entered the room.

Abdul looked up, his brown eyes widening, then his expression softened when he saw who approached. Dressed in coveralls, sleeves pushed up to his elbows, he was working with the orchids.

"How are the specimens?" asked Brent as he stopped to look at the brightly colored *oncidiums*, *dendrobiums* and *phalaenopsis* orchids growing under florescent lights.

"I thought about it and realized we needed to take more precautions, so I decided to harvest tissue from each variety," Abdul said, black hair mussed into near spikes, his slightly hooked nose smudged with soil.

"Great idea," said Brent. "How are you going about it exactly?"

"I take several slices from each specimen's leaves and slide them into these plastic tubes." He held one up for Brent to see.

"I trust you. No one knows orchids the way you do."

"I'm going to take them home where I can keep an eye on them," said Abdul. He began labeling vials and putting them in a small refrigerator. "How was your flight?" he asked Brent as he worked.

"Smooth. Any more unsettling activity out there?"

"Not the last time I looked. We haven't been to that area where the Venus flytraps are, so I'm thinking we make our way there next."

When Abdul finished, they left the station. Brent locked the door behind them, then slid the key into his front pocket. He looked up at the sky, noting that the afternoon sun had already started to dip. "I say we take the ATVs, so we make good time," he said. "We have about two hours until dark."

They headed to the north shore, the ATVs puncturing the quiet afternoon. Birds startled as they traveled, some swooping up and over them. Several deer leapt away right before they came to a marshy spot. Brent slowed, then stopped his ATV, turning off the engine. Abdul came up behind him and did the same.

Silent as they walked, they headed over the bluff and proceeded down a pathway. Brent exhaled, relieved to see the plants still intact. Then he saw what looked like a piece of red material. He glanced at Abdul and pointed as they neared it, then Abdul gasped. Brent followed his gaze to see a woman lying on her back, her face to the sky, eyes open and lifeless.

10

Brent stared at the woman, speechless.

Finally, Abdul said, "We need to call the police."

Brent shook his head. "This is federal land. I'll call my contact at the FBI." He dialed Savannah, whose phone went to voicemail. He left a message.

"Now what?" asked Abdul. "We can't just leave her out here. The animals will get her."

"How about we check the area until my contact returns the call?"

They walked through the tall grass to the edge of the marsh, where a massive grouping of carnivorous Venus flytraps grew. Brent could see immediately that the area had been disturbed.

"What do you think?" he asked Abdul.

"Someone has been here. Look how the grass has been trampled. And several bare spots where plants were pulled up."

Brent's cell phone rang then. Savannah.

"You said it was urgent?"

"Yes, Abdul and I are out in the field in the national forest and came across a body."

"A dead body?"

"Yes, a woman."

"Did you call anyone?"

"No, I figured since this is federal land it would be the FBI's jurisdiction."

"You would be right," said Savannah. "I'll get a team out there before it gets dark. Give me the coordinates."

After Brent described where they were, Savannah added, "Are there signs of anyone else out there right now?"

Brent looked at the woman's rigid face. "We appear to be alone. And I'm no expert, but I'd say she has been dead for a day or so."

"Okay, sit tight," said Savannah. "The agents should arrive in about fifteen minutes via helicopter."

Savannah slid her phone into her purse as she lifted her dark blue bag off the carousel at the airport in Atlanta. She thought about Brent and felt a rush of concern for him. It was a good thing she'd be there tomorrow. She wheeled her suitcase out of the airport into the cold, rainy weather to wave down a taxi.

Once headed for the hospital, she dialed her mother's number.

"You here?"

"Yes. I should be at the hospital in about thirty minutes. How is he?" Savannah waited for the answer, her stomach clenching.

"A lot better, but he'll appreciate seeing you."

After she hung up, Savannah looked out the window, the scenery racing by in a haze. She pulled her coat tighter around her. As she watched raindrops splatter the side of the window, she realized how worn out she felt. Though she always imagined herself a career veteran with the Bureau, the lack of respect for human life—it ate at her. The feeling had started after Jaime's death. She put a finger on the foggy taxi window and ran it through the moisture. She knew she had to let go of what happened to him and move on. She just had no idea how to go about doing so.

The helicopter set down in a nearby clearing, and a man and woman soon approached Brent and Abdul. The woman, short and sturdy with cropped black hair, gave them a quick smile and flashed her FBI badge. "I'm Agent Lorenzo and this is our medical examiner, Dr. Petros," she said.

The doctor, tall and reedy with glasses, held a black bag and glanced around.

Brent pointed to the body, and the man nodded and headed that way.

"I'd like you to both wait," said Agent Lorenzo. "I'm going to have some questions for you."

Brent and Abdul stayed put as she went to speak to the doctor and took photos, then checked out the surrounding area. Finally, she returned and opened a notebook. "I understand one of you is Brent Larson?"

"I am."

"You discovered the body?" she asked, scribbling on the notepad, then meeting his eyes.

"We both did, about an hour ago when we arrived to check on some plants. This is Abdul Farran. I work for the US Forest Service, and he works for the National Wildlife Federation. Though he's currently based here."

The agent's face remained expressionless as she made notes. "Did you see anyone else in the area? Anything out of the ordinary?"

"Just the dead body," said Brent.

"And some plants have been poached," added Abdul.

"Plants?"

"Yes, rare plants, near the marsh," Abdul gestured. "From what I can tell, a couple of groupings of the carnivorous plant *Dionaea muscipula*."

At the woman's blank look, he added, "Venus Flytrap. The plants eat flies and other insects. They are endemic only to North and South Carolina where they grow wild."

She raised her eyebrows, then scribbled some more in the notebook. "My kids had a Venus flytrap once. I had no idea they were from here." She shut the book and slid it into her pocket. "Thank you. Agent Sanchez will be in touch."

She and the medical examiner put the woman's body on a stretcher and headed for the helicopter.

"Please watch out for the plants on the path," Abdul cried after them. He looked at Brent frustrated.

When Agent Lorenzo turned and gave him a confused look, he explained, "The plants. They are rare and endangered."

She nodded and hurried ahead.

Soon the propellers chopped through the humid air, and the helicopter lifted, hovering momentarily, then heading away from the clearing. Brent and Abdul mounted their ATVs as sunset gave way to night. Their headlights punctured the thick, green growth of forest terrain as they rode back to the station.

When they parked the ATVs, Brent turned to Abdul, who appeared defeated. "This is a lot to process," he told him. "You want to come in and grab a cup of coffee before you head home?"

Abdul shook his head. "My wife's family is coming for dinner tonight. You're invited if you like?"

Brent smiled. "Maybe next time. I'm going to stay here and get some work done."

Abdul looked into the dark forest, his expression anxious. "Please be careful."

After Abdul drove off, Brent stood in the quiet of dusk. He knew he should probably be more concerned, given what they'd seen today, but the forest had always calmed him. It was to the woods that he fled when the rest of the world was topsy-turvy. The forest was the reason he'd become a ranger.

"You want to do what, son?"

"He wants to be a forest ranger," said Becky, unable to contain her enthusiasm for her brother's decision. "You know how he likes to hang out in the woods all the time. Now he can get paid to do that."

Brent's parents were sitting by the fire in their Poolesville home. They looked at one another without saying anything, then back at Brent.

His mother spoke first. "You have always loved nature, the woods, and animals. Ever since you were a boy."

Brent turned to his father, who remained contemplative, then finally spoke. "What sort of a degree do you need for this?"

"I'm planning on getting my bachelor's in forestry and environmental science, then my master's degree. I'd like to get a job with the US Forest Service. The higher my degree, the better chance I have."

"A government job isn't a bad idea," said his father, looking toward his wife. "You appear to have thought this through, son. You've always had your head on straight. We trust your judgment. You have our blessing."

Brent thought about the job responsibilities he had agreed to as a forest ranger when he signed up a decade before. Up until now, he'd been primarily dealing with trail maintenance, fire prevention, and insect control. But when he took the job, he had also agreed to protect the forestland from misuses, such as littering and poaching. In school, poaching seemed like a theoretical concept. That clearly wasn't the case anymore.

11

Brent woke up the following morning to the sound of someone rapping on his door. He checked the clock. Eight am. He rarely got visitors to his cabin. Sliding quickly out of bed, he pulled on his jeans, then climbed down the ladder from the loft and looked for a weapon. He grabbed the fireplace poker and called out, "Who is it?"

"Savannah."

Relieved, he replaced the poker and pulled open the door. She stood on his steps all business, her blonde hair offset by a tailored black suit. She wore a long, blue scarf around her neck and black leather gloves. Her eyes went to his bare chest, then back to his face. He saw her flush, and she looked away, but not before her eyes took in another glance.

"I'm sorry to bother you so early, but I just got in," she said. "I figured the sooner we move on all of this, the better." She readjusted her purse strap on one shoulder.

"We?" Brent looked behind her but didn't see anyone.

"I thought you might want to go to the coroners with me regarding Bruce. That is, if you have time. Then you could show me the area where you found the woman yesterday."

"Of course. I'll make time," said Brent. "Please come in."

Savannah walked into the main room of the cabin and glanced around, nodding in approval. "Great place."

Brent followed her gaze around the small living area with the couch and single overstuffed chair in front of the wood-burning stove, beyond that his galley kitchen. He'd had the cabin built to feature a 360-degree view of the forest from strategically placed bay windows. Through the glass he could always see the trees, lush and green, and when he opened the windows, he could hear the babble of a nearby brook.

"Thank you. I enjoy it," he said. "Just let me get dressed, then we can head out."

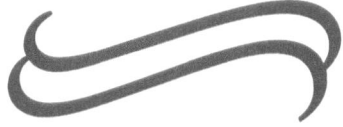

Savannah surveyed Brent's tidy cabin, impressed with how well he utilized the space. Across the room, titles lined his bookshelf, Edward Abbey, Henry David Thoreau, and Rick Bass. A quote, burned into wood, hung on one wall: "The idea of wilderness needs no defense, it only needs defenders." Her eye went to a collection of bird feathers placed in a glass jelly jar on a top shelf. In the kitchen, three cast-iron skillets of varying sizes hung on one wall, and on shelves above the sink he had stacked earthenware bowls and plates. Work boots stood by the front door, caked in mud. Savannah walked over to the window and gazed out at the scenery. A cottontail rabbit hopped by and disappeared into the underbrush. She smiled. Everything about the place felt so peaceful.

Brent emerged from his overhead loft, a fresh blue and

brown plaid shirt on, his hair combed back, slightly wet. "Ready when you are," he said as he grabbed his jacket.

In the car, they headed toward the main highway. "How long have you lived here?" Savannah asked.

"Since I took the post as a ranger, so ten years now. How long have you worked for the FBI?"

"Going on eleven years in July," she said.

"Do you like it?"

Savannah thought for a moment. "I do. Usually. When I catch the bad guys." She reached up and adjusted the rearview mirror.

"You always work alone?"

Savannah's stomach tightened, then she took a deep breath. "I used to work with a partner, but he died in the line of duty."

"I'm sorry to hear that."

Savannah liked how Brent didn't probe like most people did when she mentioned Jaime. Instead, he stayed quiet, looking out the window.

After a time, she said, "I would ask if you like your work with the forest service, but it's obvious you do."

Brent laughed. "I'm pretty transparent."

"That's not a bad thing."

"Unless you're trying to play something close to the vest," he replied. "I've never been very good at hiding my intentions."

Savannah sped up to pass a truck pulling a trailer, then replied, "Given that I spend my days dealing with people always trying to hide something, I find that refreshing."

Brent didn't reply, but out of the corner of her eye, Savannah could see a small smile form on his lips.

. . .

They arrived at the coroner's a little after nine. Savannah showed her credentials at the front desk and introduced Brent as Patterson's colleague. Then they walked down a short corridor and came to the door of the morgue. Savannah turned to Brent. "You can wait outside if you prefer."

He shook his head. "I'll be fine."

Savannah took a breath. Death had a way of making her feel as if each time was the first.

The frigid room contained several gurneys, most with bodies on them. At one of the gurneys, the medical examiner, a headlamp on her head, examined the corpse of a woman. She looked up and raised her eyebrows as they approached.

"I'm Agent Sanchez. I called about the autopsy of Bruce Patterson."

The woman nodded. "I'm glad you called." She took the lamp off her head and set it on a nearby empty gurney. Then she walked over to a cluttered desk in the corner and picked up a file.

"Turns out we still have the body, as there has been some back-and-forth with the family whether he's going to be buried or cremated." The ME opened the file. "Given your assessment regarding the possibility of foul play, I reviewed the autopsy findings with that in mind." She held up a finger. "It would be best if I show you what I found."

"That would be great," said Savannah.

The coroner went to the back of the room and checked the numbers on the large stainless steel metal drawers lining the wall that held the cadavers, then pulled one open and lowered the sheet covering the body to expose the face. She beckoned for them to come over.

As if sleeping, Patterson lay there, his face relaxed and drained of color. In the back of her mind, Savannah worried about Brent's reaction to the viewing of his colleague's body.

She snuck a glance at him. He stared at Patterson, then lifted his gaze.

"With the original autopsy, I had checked his stomach contents, and there was nothing suspicious. I also reviewed the tox screen, which didn't show anything. But after your call, I took another look. She pointed to Patterson's nose. "See this?"

Savannah moved closer to peer at Patterson's face. "I see a trace of white around the nose," she said. "Drugs?"

"You could say Mother Nature's drugs. *Nerium* up the nose. Most likely forced."

"He was poisoned with oleander?"

"Looks that way."

"So, the killer knows their way around plants," said Savannah. The smell of formaldehyde was getting to her.

"Most definitely," said the coroner as she pushed Patterson's body back into the slot. "My guess is that it was a concentrated form distilled by the killer. It could have been administered with a handkerchief, even."

Savannah looked at Brent, whose face had gone white. "You okay?" She moved toward him. "I'm sorry, this can be unpleasant. You want to sit down?"

Brent nodded. "That might be a good idea."

The coroner pulled out the chair from her desk and Brent sat, then took several deep breaths. After a moment, he said, "The hardest part is knowing someone poisoned him. I can't imagine what kind of a death that must have been. If only I'd talked to him that day."

Savannah laid a hand on his arm. "Whoever wanted him dead was determined to make that happen. There was nothing you could do, so don't beat yourself up." As she said that Jaime's face flashed before her. How many times had she told herself those very same words?

12

As they left the coroner's office, Brent couldn't help replaying his and Bruce's last conversation in his head. When they walked out of the building and were heading to the car, Savannah looked up at a darkening sky. "Best we get to the site where you found the body before rain washes away any evidence," she said.

Brent shook the memory of the last time he'd seen Bruce out of his head and answered. "We'll need to take the ATVs."

A half hour later, they were racing toward the marsh, Brent's ATV in the lead. When they came upon the area, he slowed to a crawl, checking carefully on both sides of the ATV to not run over any plants. He stopped the vehicle and hopped off.

Savannah pulled up behind him and climbed off the ATV, appearing amazingly unruffled for someone who had just taken a fast ride through marshland. She had put her long hair in a braid and wore hiking boots she'd pulled from her car before they departed.

"Show me where the body was," she said.

Brent led her to the edge of the marsh and pointed to the spot a few feet away.

She went over and crouched down and examined the area. Brent could see an impression where the grass was still matted from the body. Finally, he broke the silence. "See anything?"

She stood up. "About how many pounds would you say the woman was?"

Brent recalled the body. "Maybe one-hundred-twenty pounds?"

Savannah took the backpack she wore off and removed a tape measure. Then she carefully inserted the tape into the indentation in multiple places. She studied the measurements for a few minutes, then spoke, "The indentation is much deeper than would occur for someone of that weight."

"That suggests what?"

"Let me check on something." She took out her cell phone and dialed. "Yeah, Sanchez here. You have a COD on the Jane Doe found at the marsh yet?"

Brent heard talking on the other end of the line, then Savannah said, "Okay, thank you." She hung up the phone and faced him. "As I suspected from the measurements, her cause of death is strangulation." Brent must have given her a puzzled look because she continued. "Someone was on top of her, strangling her, likely someone with some weight, so probably a male."

"Does that information help?" asked Brent.

"It actually brings up more questions. Strangulation and poisoning are very different MOs, which suggests two different perpetrators."

Raindrops started to fall then.

"Are we good to go?" asked Brent.

Savannah nodded and got back on the ATV, turning on the engine and revving it. He followed her as she raced along, expertly traveling around vegetation and leading them without incident to the ranger station. When they arrived, he pointed to the barn, and they drove in and stopped the engines. By now, the rain was beating a steady rhythm on the tin roof.

"Doesn't look like we're going to get a break anytime soon," said Brent. "Ready to run for the station?"

Savannah nodded and Brent turned and sprinted through the rain, Savannah at his heels. When they got to the small porch, he unlocked the door. Inside the entryway, they dripped water onto the floor mat as Brent reached over to turn on the lights. "Looks like Abdul hasn't come in yet today. I'll have to turn on the heater."

Savannah wrapped her arms around herself. "I like that idea."

"I've got a change of clothing for you if you want. We have laundry facilities where we can dry our clothes."

"I like that idea, too." She followed him into a back room, where he opened his locker and extracted clothing for the both of them. Handing her a pair of his slacks and a sweatshirt, he said, "These are obviously going to be too big on you, but they'll keep you warm. I'll leave so you can change."

Brent shut the door behind himself. He went to the men's room and stripped out of his wet clothing and put on dry ones, then he turned the thermostat up. Savannah came out of the locker room with her wet clothing in hand. She had rolled the pant legs up, and his sweatshirt reached to her knees. Out of the braid, her hair fell down her back in damp rivulets. At the sight of her, Brent felt a rush of excitement.

"I hope you don't mind, but I found a tie in your locker that I used for a belt," she said.

Brent smiled. "Resourceful. To be honest, that tie hasn't been used for years. I wore it my first day as a ranger. If you accidentally took it home with you that would be okay."

Savannah laughed for the first time since they'd met, her green eyes lighting up. "You don't seem like the tie type," she said.

He must have given her a funny look because she frowned. "Did I say something?"

"I was just thinking that it was nice to hear you laugh. You probably don't do that much in your line of work."

Savannah studied Brent's face for a moment as if she were gauging his reason for the comment. Then her shoulders relaxed. "You're right. And there's not many people I laugh with."

Brent wanted to ask about the people in her life but instead said, "How about I throw our clothing in the dryer and then we have something hot to drink?"

"That sounds good. I'll take black tea if you have any."

Brent pointed down the hall to the kitchen. "Have a seat in there. I'll be right back to make us some."

He went into the utility room and threw their clothing in the dryer, then made his way to the kitchen where he found Savannah sitting at the kitchen table.

Brent opened a cupboard and pulled out a box of black tea.

"Two bags if you don't mind. I like it strong," said Savannah.

Brent nodded while he filled the teakettle, then lit the range as lightning flashed outside of a nearby window. Seconds later, thunder rumbled.

"I'm glad we got out of the rain when we did," commented Brent, peering out to see tree limbs begin to thrash in the wind. After pouring steaming water into two earthenware mugs, he carried them to the table, along with a tray of sweeteners. He pulled up a chair across from Savannah.

She poured two packets of sugar into her tea, then

wrapped her hands around the mug and took a tentative sip. "Thank you," she said. She looked around the room at the rough-hewn walls. "So this is headquarters for you out here in the forest."

Brent nodded. "It's pretty quiet right now, but usually there's four of us, including Bruce and Abdul. We have a junior ranger, but she's on a short sabbatical for an arboriculture class in Ohio." At the reminder of Abdul, Brent checked his cell phone. No messages.

"Something the matter?" asked Savannah.

"Abdul is usually in by now," he said.

"It is storming out there."

"True, but the weather rarely stops him. Excuse me for a second." He pushed the number on his phone for Abdul. Straight to voicemail. "No answer," he said, unease slithering through him.

Savannah set down her mug, concern on her face.

"Maybe I should call his wife to see if she has seen him."

"Let's not alarm her unduly. I'll have headquarters trace his phone's location, and his car."

Brent gave her Abdul's number and make and model of his car. He waited while Savannah made the call and requested the information. A minute later, Brent heard someone come back on the line as Savannah's brow furrowed.

13

Savannah hung up the phone. "Abdul's phone is pinging here," she said.

Brent set down his cup. "Here, as in the ranger station?"

"Somewhere in this vicinity. Is it possible he's out on the property?"

"In the rain? Not likely. Can you pinpoint where?"

Savannah checked her phone, then pointed to the back of the building. She got up from her chair, and Brent followed. "It's showing back here."

"That's where we're keeping the orchid specimens," said Brent, his heart racing at what they'd find. When he pushed open the door to the room, though, no one was there. He walked up to the counter where the specimens were lined up under lighting. Savannah came to stand beside him.

"These are the plants you saved?"

Brent nodded. "Maybe Abdul accidentally left his phone here." He checked around the counter, then glanced at the floor and spotted a phone. He motioned to lean over and pick it up, but Savannah put her hand on his forearm to stop him.

"This could be a crime scene. Let me."

Brent swallowed and stepped back. First Bruce and now Abdul? The last thing he wanted to discover was that something bad had happened to his friend. He wearily shook his head and ran his hand over his face.

Savannah took a paper towel from the dispenser on the counter and picked up the phone. "Does this look like his?"

Brent eyed a small indentation on one corner where Abdul had dropped it. "Yes, that's definitely it."

"What are the chances Abdul would leave his phone on the floor like this?"

"Zero percent."

Savannah surveyed the room, her eyes stopping on an exit door on the back wall. "Do you use that door often?"

"No, it's more of an emergency exit. Why?" Brent felt the worry rising within him.

She looked thoughtful for a moment. "I need my CSI kit from the car." Savannah turned to head out of the room.

"It's still pouring. Let me get it for you," said Brent.

"No, need. I won't melt."

Now it was Brent's turn to put his hand on her arm. "I want to feel like I'm helping in some way."

Savannah's eyes softened. "Okay. The kit is in the trunk. Dark brown bag."

Savannah watched as Brent put on a rain slicker. He didn't rush but made sure to snap up the raincoat and put the car keys in the front pocket. Then he pulled open the front door of the station, sending in a blast of cold, wet air. After he shut the door firmly behind himself, she watched through the window as a blur of bright yellow flew by. Within a minute, he was back inside, rain sliding off the slicker onto the welcome mat. He handed her the bag.

Savannah smiled. "Thank you."

"If Abdul is in trouble, I want to help," he said. "Is there anything at all I can do that might push us closer to finding him?"

"There just might be," she said over her shoulder as she headed into the back of the ranger station. Brent followed her.

Once in the room, Savannah sat down on a stool and pulled the phone toward her. "I'm going to start by dusting his phone for prints." She pulled her fingerprinting kit out of her bag. "In the meantime, check around the room for anything that looks out of place. Even the slightest thing may be of significance. But don't touch anything."

Brent did as instructed while Savannah sprinkled fine powder onto the front of Abdul's phone, then lightly twirled her brush on the screen until a couple of fingerprints emerged. She took a photo, then tapped in Cherie's email and hit send, following it up with a text to get back to her after checking AIFIS. She looked over to see Brent crouched by the doorway.

"You find something?" She slid off the stool and walked over.

Brent remained staring at the floor and replied, his voice filled with concern, "There's something red on the floor. I'm not sure, but it could be blood."

Savannah knelt to check out the area. Sure enough, it looked like blood. She went to get a collection bag, then scraped the substance off the floor with a swab and slid the swab into a test tube. After she finished, she took photos of some boot prints in the dust that covered the floor. "What size foot would you say Abdul has, and does he wear boots?"

"His foot is smaller than mine. I'd say a nine. And he usually wears tennis shoes. I've teased him about that."

Savannah stood and faced him. His eyes went to the test tube in her hand.

"It looks like blood, but it's a very minor amount," she told him. "Is there anything else out of place?"

Brent shook his head. "No, it's as if Abdul left without a trace."

"No one leaves without a trace," Savannah assured him. "There could be a perfectly logical explanation for all of this. No need to panic. Maybe his wife needed him, and he had to rush home. Best to keep a clear head."

Brent took a deep breath. "I know you're right. But after Bruce."

Savannah and Brent stood so close, she could feel the heat coming from his body. She felt the urge to take him by the arms to reassure him, but she kept her hands to herself. "I know it's hard, especially when someone has been murdered. You get skittish."

Brent's eyes were intense. "I guess you would know in your line of work," he said quietly.

She nodded slowly. "More than you know. So, let's stay positive until we know otherwise." She turned to survey the plants on the counter. Her eye went to an orchid forming a bud. She walked over to give it a closer look. "This is gorgeous. I don't think I've seen such a striking purple in an orchid. It's incredible that you've got some blooming at this time of year."

"That's Abdul's doing. He's the orchid expert. The lighting simulates real daylight, and they're growing on heating pads. He thinks these could be a species that hasn't been discovered or identified yet."

Savannah studied the scalloped edges of the orchid leaves. "The idea that this is a whole new species is really exciting," she said.

"When we met, you said that your family owns a nursery in Georgia. I guess you decided not to go into horticulture."

Savannah smiled. "It's my mama's and gramma's nursery. I used to love playing there when I was a kid, and I worked there during high school. Plants are great, but I always felt like I was supposed to do something..." she trailed off, unsure how to finish the sentence.

"More?" suggested Brent.

"No, just different," said Savannah. "Who knows. Maybe when I retire from the Bureau, I'll take over the business."

They didn't say anything for a few minutes as Savannah continued to admire the orchids. Then Brent broke the silence. "How about something to eat while we wait on word about Abdul?"

"That would be great," said Savannah. "All I had for breakfast was a cardboard muffin on the plane."

"I've got some lentil soup. Homemade by Abdul's wife."

"Sounds wonderful."

Savannah followed Brent to the kitchen, admiring his muscular backside as a flush of warmth swept through her. It'd been a long time since a man had affected her like that.

14

Savannah took her last spoonful of lentil soup when her phone rang. She checked the screen. It was her mama.

"Excuse me," she said, then answered. "What's up? Grampa okay?"

"He sure is. Looks like the stroke was minor. But scared him enough to hopefully start taking better care of himself. Or at least that's what your gramma hopes."

"Well, that's good news. Tell him I love him."

"I'm also calling about the photos you sent."

Savannah set down her spoon. "What do you think?"

"My Lord, I haven't seen anything like it, to be honest. And I've seen a lot of orchids. I don't think they're *dendrobiums*. I honestly don't know what they are. The thing that's got me most puzzled is the foliage. As you know, foliage is how a lot of plants are classified."

"So, a hybrid of some sort?"

"Yes, but likely one made by Mother Nature. I'm sorry I can't be of much help, honey."

"Thanks, Mama. That does help," said Savannah, who met Brent's eyes. "I'll call later."

"What did she say about the orchids?" he asked when she hung up.

"She agrees that the orchids aren't like anything she's ever seen, so most likely a whole new species."

The walls of the ranger station shook as thunder continued to rumble outside. Brent glanced up at the ceiling at the area he had patched after last fall's rain. Still holding. Then he watched Savannah as she picked up her mug of tea.

"You said murder was no stranger to you," he said softly. "You're speaking about your profession, right? Nothing personal?" He immediately regretted his question when Savannah, about to take a sip of tea, stopped with the mug midair.

"I'm sorry. It seemed there might be more to it," he said. "Not my business. I'm worried about Abdul, and I..." He struggled to give her an explanation. In truth, it was the solemn way she had looked at him, a darkness clouding her face at her own words. Even now she appeared to be blinking back tears.

Savannah set her mug down and frowned, then took a deep breath. "The truth is...well, things happen. What I mean is." She ran her fingertip around the rim of the tea mug. "Of course, I've seen a lot of murders in the ten years I've been on the job, but you're right, I also have personal experience."

"Like I said, it's not a question you need to answer if you don't want to," said Brent, getting up.

Savannah held up a hand to stop him. "It's okay." She took

another breath, her eyes on his. "My husband was murdered five years ago."

Shit, thought Brent, shocked at her words. He had really stepped into it. He waited, unsure of how to respond.

Savannah brushed her hair back from her face. "His name was Jaime. We were partners with the Bureau until things got personal." Savannah shifted in her seat. "We stopped being partners once we got married, and he went into another division."

No wonder she didn't smile much, thought Brent, as he watched her face. She remained stoic, but he could tell she was struggling. When she didn't say anything more, he said quietly. "It was in the line of duty? His murder?"

She nodded, her eyes bright. "Yes."

"I'm very sorry," said Brent, wishing he hadn't brought it up.

Savannah sat up straighter. "It's not your fault, but I appreciate it." She took a napkin and dabbed beneath her lower lashes.

Savannah couldn't believe she had just told Brent about Jaime's murder. But he did ask, and he was easy to talk to.

Brent looked at her thoughtfully. "Thank you for sharing that with me."

Savannah smiled slightly. "I don't know if I'd be thanking me if I was you. I know you're worried about Abdul. I'm sure that revelation didn't help. We'll figure out where he is," she assured him.

"I believe you," said Brent. He motioned with his chin to her empty bowl. "You done?"

She nodded. "It was good. Thank you."

Savannah watched as he set the bowls in the sink and turned on the water. She picked up her phone and checked the screen. Nothing from Cherie yet. Brent came back to the table to sit across from her, but she kept her eyes on the phone. She hoped he wasn't going to ask anything else about Jaime.

"Should we check in with Abdul's wife?" he asked.

"Given what we found in the orchid room," said Savannah, "it would be good to know when she last saw him."

Brent pulled his phone out of his pocket. He was about to dial, then stopped. "What should I say?"

"Just ask if Abdul is with her. See what she says."

Brent nodded and dialed. Savannah heard the phone ringing, then a woman's voice.

"Hi, Aadhila, it's Brent. "Is Abdul there?"

Savannah waited as Brent mouthed no.

"Okay. I'm calling because he left his cell phone at work. When was the last time you talked to him?" Another brief pause. "He's probably just out at one of the sites. I'll have him call you when he gets in."

Brent hung up. "She saw him this morning. He said he had to get to the station early but didn't tell her why."

"That's good news," Savannah said when she saw doubt on Brent's face. "It means he hasn't been missing for very long. Or, like you said, he could just be out checking on plants. I've walked off and left my phone more than once."

Brent was about to reply when Savannah's phone rang. She checked the screen. Cherie. "Just a sec," she said, pressing the button to answer.

"Boss, I've got news about Farran's car."

"I'm listening," said Savannah.

"Local PD found it on the side of the road. Looks like there was a struggle. I told them to hold off until you got there. I'll text you the coordinates. Also, no hits in IAFIS for the fingerprints on the phone. We do have an ID on the woman found at the marsh, though. Victoria Hunter. She was an environmental activist."

"News about Abdul?" asked Brent when Savannah hung up the phone.

She took a deep breath. "The police found his car on the side of the road."

"Was he there?" He clenched his fists as he asked.

"No sign of him, but they're waiting until I get there to check out the scene."

Brent stood. "I'm going with you. I'm sure our clothes are dry by now." As he headed out of the room, Savannah decided it was pointless to object. She just hoped the scene wasn't a bloody one.

15

As Savannah drove, Brent crossed his arms over his chest, willing the panic down. How had everything gone so wrong so quickly?

Savannah slowed the car to a crawl as they approached a squad car with flashing lights parked next to Abdul's vehicle. Two cops in rain slickers stood talking to each other. She stopped on the shoulder and turned the engine off. "I'm sorry, but maybe it would be better if you stay here while I check out what's going on first."

Everything in Brent wanted to get out of the car and go see what had happened, but he said, "Fine. I don't want to get in the way."

Savannah put her hand out to touch his arm. "I just want to assess what happened as quickly as possible. I'll be back soon to update you. We'll find him."

Brent met Savannah's eyes, which were sincere, and relaxed his arm. "Thank you."

After pulling a compact, black umbrella from the glove box, Savannah opened the door, welcoming in a spray of cold raindrops. Then she hopped out and slammed the car door, hurrying to Abdul's car. She talked briefly with the officers, then pointed to Abdul's trunk. The officer shook his head, then went around to the front of the car, and the trunk popped open. Brent watched with his heart in his throat as Savannah raised it and peered inside. She leaned over and rummaged around, then slammed the trunk shut. Brent let out a breath he didn't realize he'd been holding. When she headed for the front of the car, he felt his cell phone buzzing in his pants pocket. He pulled the phone out and checked the screen. *Unknown caller.* His heart hammering in his ears, he answered. "Hello?"

"Brent, it's Abdul."

Brent sat up in the car, relief flooding through him. "Are you okay?"

"I'm okay, but..." The man sounded as if he were in pain.

"Where are you?" Brent's voice rose.

"I need you to bring the rest of the plants to me," said Abdul. He hesitated for a moment, as if he needed his friend to realize the weight of his words. "If you don't...." Brent waited, his ears straining. He heard voices he couldn't make out. "If you don't, they're going to kill me." A deadly silence hung between them.

"Abdul! Who is they?"

"Tomorrow at four pm. They'll send you the coordinates. It's important you come alone. Tell no one." Then he was gone.

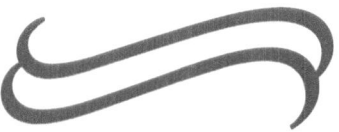

Savannah surveyed the scene. Even though it was raining, she could tell there had been a struggle, indicated by the deep indentations in the wet soil next to the car. She also spied a set of nearby tire prints quickly degrading in the rain. They looked large, most likely a truck or van. She took some photos with her phone before they were completely obliterated. Then she returned to Abdul's car and opened the driver's side door. If she recalled, he was a short statured man. But the seat had been pushed back to the max, which meant he wasn't the one driving before the car was abandoned. She would have them tow the vehicle back to the local FBI facility, so their team could dust and inspect the interior. After slamming the door before the rain compromised any more evidence, she instructed the officer to wait until the FBI tow truck came and retrieved it. Then she surveyed the surrounding landscape for any signs of life, but it was impossible to get a clear view through the rain. She trudged back to the car, the wind pulling on the umbrella as she walked.

When she got in the car and slipped her umbrella next to her in the door, she turned to Brent. "No one in the car, although it looks like there was a struggle." She examined his face, which held an odd expression. "That's good news," she continued. "If they wanted him dead, they would have killed him and left him here." She waited for a response, but none came. "Like I told you, we'll find him," she assured him, starting up the car and hoping she was right. "I'm going to head to your house so we can strategize our next step."

When they arrived at his cabin, Savannah turned off the car and said, "These people have given us an ultimatum by taking Abdul." She turned toward him. "It's up to us to decide what happens next. Are you okay with that?"

"Whatever it takes to get Abdul out in one piece. I fear what their next step will be."

"Then let's try to be one step ahead of their thinking," she said. "Which means we might be forced to take a few risks."

Savannah put her hand on the door handle to open it, when Brent said, "Wait."

"What is it?"

"When you were outside, I got a call from an unknown number. It was Abdul."

"What did he say?"

"He sounded like he might be hurt, and he told me to bring all of the orchids to a yet to be disclosed location tomorrow afternoon."

"Anything else?"

Brent swallowed. "To tell no one at all and to come alone or they would kill him."

"I'm glad you told me. I can't tell you how often people try to go it alone with kidnappings, and things go horribly wrong."

Brent ran his hands through his hair. "This is Abdul's life. I figure you know a lot more about this than I do, but don't we have to do what they say?"

"We can make it seem like you're doing what they say, but you'll have backup," she said. Then she eyed his cabin. "Your placed could be bugged. I'm going to get my kit and check it out."

16

After a thorough sweep of Brent's cabin showed no monitoring devices, Savannah opened the front door and announced, "All clear."

Brent entered, taking off his jacket and hanging it on a hook by the door. Then he headed for the small kitchen and opened a cupboard above the refrigerator, reaching for a bottle. "I'm not much of a drinker, but right now I feel like a glass of my dad's scotch." He set the bottle on the counter and opened another cupboard with glasses, then glanced over his shoulder at Savannah. "Want some?"

"I normally don't drink on duty, but a small glass won't hurt," she told him. She slid out of her jacket and hung it on the hook next to Brent's. As she did so, she randomly wondered if anyone else ever used the second hook, like another woman. Then she turned and took the tumbler he extended to her and followed him to the sitting area where he plunked the bottle down on the table between them.

Savannah took a swallow of the smooth, amber liquid, then eyed the bottle. It didn't have a label. "That's a good scotch, malty, with nice finish. You said it was your dad's? How long has it aged?"

"It's about a decade old, I think," he said. "My dad distilled as a hobby." He took another swallow and swirled his glass, glancing out the window. Savannah followed his gaze to see the storm beginning to lift in the waning gray light.

"I know this is tough," she said after a few moments. "But my team and I have a good track record when it comes to kidnapping cases, if that helps."

Brent set the glass down on the table. "It does, actually."

Savannah gave him what she hoped was an encouraging smile. "Good. I'm going to make some phone calls to set things up for tomorrow."

An hour later, Savannah had arranged to get her team in from DC so they could help coordinate Brent's handoff of the orchids the next afternoon. She also readied her laptop for tracing if Abdul called again, after sending an agent to his home to watch over his wife and family.

Brent, who had been silent for most of the time, finally spoke when she hung up the phone with Cherie. "You just mentioned someone named Wallen. Is his first name Jack?"

Savannah set down her phone. "Yes, he ran me off the road the night I left your house in Poolesville. You know him?"

Brent's face became serious. "I went to school with him." He refilled his glass and took a drink. "We were friends for a while. His family had problems, and they didn't have a lot of money, so he made extra cash doing odd jobs for my folks."

"It looks like his odd jobs have turned into illegal activities, like armed robbery and burglary," said Savannah.

"Do you think he's involved with Abdul's abduction?"

"It's possible. Have you spoken to him recently?"

"Not for several years. I could ask my sister."

Savannah shook her head. "Your sister lives in LA, right? Let's just leave her out of this for now."

Brent nodded. "So now what?"

"Look, I don't feel good about leaving you alone overnight. If it's okay with you, I'd like to stay here."

"That's not necessary, Savannah. I'll be fine."

"I don't think I would sleep all night worrying if someone is scouting around out there in the dark."

"I don't have a guest room," he said.

"This couch is pretty comfortable. I insist, okay?"

Brent looked thoughtful. "On one condition. If you help put fresh linens on my bed, and I take the couch."

Savannah opened her mouth to refuse, but Brent stopped her. "It's nonnegotiable."

Savannah laughed. "I've slept on much worse than a couch, believe me."

Brent smiled for the first time in hours. "Okay, that's settled. How about I make us something for dinner?" he suggested, changing the subject. He stood, and she was once again taken by his impressive stature.

It took her a couple of beats to answer. "How about I help? I'm a pretty good cook."

"Pretty good works," said Brent, who headed for the kitchen and pulled open the refrigerator. "I've got some ground beef. We could make spaghetti."

Savannah thought about the spaghetti she never got to eat at her sister's house. "I think that sounds perfect."

They spent the next hour together chopping onions and garlic, browning the ground beef, and making a skillet of sauce from scratch. While the spaghetti noodles boiled, Brent took some romaine lettuce out of the fridge, and Savannah washed it while he cut up carrots and cucumber. As they worked, they talked about nothing in particular. Savannah realized she missed such everyday moments with a man. At one point when Brent had to reach over her to grab Italian seasoning from the cupboard, he stopped momentarily and looked at her. What was he thinking?

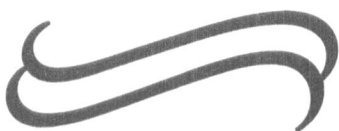

Though Abdul filled his thoughts, Brent found comfort in making dinner with Savannah. She kept her guard up, her eyes sweeping the outdoors periodically and checking her phone, but she also became lighthearted at times, especially when she spoke about her nephew.

"It must be fun to watch a little one grow up," said Brent. "I bet he admires his aunt the FBI agent."

"Actually, the little rascal is quite irreverent." Savannah fished a spaghetti noodle out of the boiling water and let it cool on the end of a fork before sampling. "He calls me Aunt Savannah Banana, and the last time I saw him he wanted me to teach him how to pick a lock."

Brent laughed and brought a colander to the kitchen sink where Savannah poured in the noodles to drain. Then he pulled out a bottle of red wine from the cupboard and held it up. "Would you like a glass?" he asked.

"Yes, thank you."

When they had fragrant piles of spaghetti on their plates and sat down to enjoy the meal, Savannah dug in with gusto.

"I take it our sauce is good?" he asked, taking a bite himself.

She finished chewing. "Delicious. I didn't realize how hungry I was."

Brent held up his glass of wine. "To our sauce."

They ate in comfortable silence for a time, both clearing their plates. Brent was about to ask if she wanted seconds when his cell phone rang. Savannah shot up from the table and grabbed her laptop, quickly attaching his phone to the computer with a cord. "Go ahead and answer," she said. "Keep him on as long as possible."

Brent nodded and answered with the speaker phone. "Abdul?"

"This isn't Abdul," said a man's deep voice.

"Where is he? Is he okay?"

"For the moment, yes, but he won't be for long if you don't do exactly what you're told."

"Let me talk to Abdul," demanded Brent as a heated anger seeped through his body.

"You're in no position to bargain, Mr. Larson. Now listen carefully. You have been sent coordinates. Gather all, and I mean all, of the orchids from the ranger station and bring them to the location tonight at midnight."

Brent looked at Savannah as panic surfaced. "I thought I was going to bring you the plants tomorrow. Why the sudden change of plans?"

"Don't be late," the man demanded, then the phone went dead.

17

"Did you get the location?" asked Brent when the man hung up.

Savannah shook her head. "I needed four more seconds. This guy knows what he's doing."

"Now what?"

Savannah held up a finger, then dialed her phone and spoke when someone answered. "We've got a situation. The kidnapper wants a meet tonight." Brent could hear a voice on the other end and watched Savannah frown. "Okay, we'll make do." She hung up and set the phone on the table.

"Make do? That doesn't sound good," said Brent.

"With the pushed-up deadline, my agents aren't going to be in place in time. They're on their way to the airport, but there's no way they'll make it." She began tapping a foot on the floor. "I could call in the local LEOs, but I don't think that's a good idea since the caller made it clear he wants you to come alone."

"Local LEOs?" Brent asked.

"Sorry, lingo. Law enforcement officers." She stood up and began pacing. "I'll suit you up in a bulletproof vest, and

I'll be there with you out of sight. You can do the handoff; I'll back you up."

Brent put his head in his hands, then raised his eyes to meet Savannah's. "What if something goes wrong?"

She held his gaze, her voice level. "There's always that chance, but if we're smart and careful, we should be able to get through this. I've been in situations like this before. And though I'd rather have my team backing us up, in some ways this is better. If this guy is as smart as he seems, he might sense something." She reached over and put her hand on Brent's. "The most important thing is that we get Abdul back unharmed."

She seemed confident, Brent thought, as if she knew exactly what to do. His first thought was that without her they were screwed. She was the only possibility Abdul had to survive. Brent nodded his head slowly. "Okay, tell me what to do."

They headed to the ranger station to collect the plants. Brent brought a sterile container to put them in, though at first, he wasn't sure why he cared, since he'd be giving the rare specimens away to thieves. But he would do whatever was needed to make certain the orchids survived. Inside the station, he took the plants from their controlled environment on the heating pads and carefully put each pot in separate compartments.

"We'll get this bastard," she said, watching him, "and save the plants, too."

Brent paused, a lime-green orchid with burgundy splotches on the petals in his hand. "Abdul would like that." His stomach wrenched when he thought how his actions tonight would affect his colleague's fate.

After the plants were secured for transport, Savannah

handed Brent a bulletproof vest. "This guy is unpredictable," she said. "It's best we're prepared."

Brent eyed the vest, which was heavier than he imagined. "Is this yours?"

"Yes, but it should fit you."

"What about you?"

"You can't go in there without protection. Put it on underneath your shirt," she instructed.

Brent thought about protesting, then decided just to follow her lead. To help Abdul, he had to stay alive, and she certainly had more experience in circumstances like these than he did. He unbuttoned his shirt and slid it off, then feeling as if he were moving in slow motion, pulled on the vest.

"It's pretty easy to secure," she said. "but let me know if you need help."

The idea of Savannah helping him with his vest had a certain appeal, but he managed to secure it and put his shirt back on. The vest was cumbersome and restricted his movement, but he felt safer knowing it protected his vital organs. Whatever lay ahead, he would have to follow his own intuition.

At eleven o'clock, they headed out in Brent's car. The sky was a flat, dark blue, the moon obscured by a layer of clouds. Savannah sat in the back seat, saying she would hide herself when they got to the meet. "Remember," she said as Brent drove. "I'll be right here, my gun ready. Demand that they produce Abdul and that he comes to the car first before you will get the plants out."

"What if they don't have him? Is there a plan for what I do?" asked Brent.

"The most important thing is your life. Run back to the

car. I'll be covering you. We're gambling on the knowledge that they want the plants far more than they want Abdul. We have to believe they're not going to do anything to jeopardize that."

Brent glanced in the rearview mirror and met her eyes. Drawing his attention back to the road, he read an upcoming sign. "Forrester is coming up," he said.

"I'm going to get on the floor of the car," said Savannah. "Drive in slow. If it looks like an ambush, turn around and hightail it out of there."

"Ambush?" said Brent.

"I'm just bringing up a possibility," said Savannah in a steady voice. She was silent a moment. "You'll be fine."

Brent peered up ahead. "It's pitch black. I can't see anything."

"Don't talk anymore. You don't want to make it look like there's someone in the car with you."

Brent kept his eyes straight ahead. Finally, he noticed what looked like headlights as he slowed the car to a crawl. When he was several yards away, he stopped and turned off the engine. His heart hammering in his temples, he saw a man standing in front of an SUV, but no Abdul. He took a deep breath, then got out of the car and shut the door. As he started to approach the man, he called out, "I'm here for Abdul."

The man, a hulking giant with a ski mask on and a gun in his hand, countered in a deep voice, "Where are the plants?"

Brent stopped in his tracks. "I'm not going to give them to you until I have Abdul."

The hulk started toward Brent, the gun pointed at his chest. "We've got a problem then."

18

Brent knew he should be heeding Savannah's instructions to return to the car, but anger flashed through him. "The deal was you'd bring Abdul, and I'd make sure you got the plants," he said as the man came to stand in front of him. "I'm not giving you the plants until you hand him over."

The gun leveled at Brent, the man said, "You're in no position to negotiate, Larson. Once we have the plants, we'll release him. I can just as easily shoot you and get them myself."

"I'm not here to screw you. This is supposed to be a fair trade. I get Abdul, you get the plants. Otherwise, this is a waste of time." Brent looked over the man's shoulder at the SUV.

The hulk suddenly reached out a large hand and grabbed Brent by the shirt. Some of the buttons popped off, exposing his torso.

"Son of a bitch!" the man yelled. "You're wearing a vest. We told you no cops."

Taking the opportunity to wrench free, Brent swung around and ran toward the car. He'd only taken a few steps when he saw Savannah jump out of the back seat and yell, "FBI. Put the gun down!"

Brent ripped the door open and dove into the car as shots rang out. He heard a grunt and a thud, then some movement. When he sat up and looked through the windshield, he saw Savannah heading for the man, who lay on his back on the ground. She reached down and checked his pulse, then walked toward the truck. His heart hammering, Brent followed and watched while she searched the vehicle.

"No signs of Abdul." She walked back to the dead man and tore his ski mask off and took a photo of his face. Then, with effort, she rolled him over and pulled a cell phone out of his back pocket. Just as she did so, it buzzed. She tried to check the text. "Phone's locked," she murmured. Squatting on the ground beside the man, she picked up his right hand, placing his forefinger on the phone, which unlocked it.

She stood and checked the screen as Brent came to look over her shoulder. It read: *Do you have the plants?*

Savannah tapped, *Yes.*

Head back to base.

She answered, *What about the hostage?*

Get back here now.

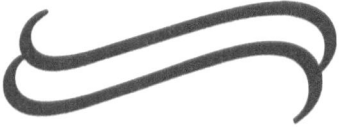

Savannah scrolled through the man's texts and noted he used the thumbs up a lot, so she replied with one.

"Now what?" Brent asked.

"I'm going to have Cherie check this number to find out where our man was last, as it's probably their basecamp. I

DISCOVERED TRANSGRESSIONS

doubt he was smart enough to delete the location, just in case. Then I'll head there to hopefully round up Abdul."

"What do you mean, you? I'm going with you."

She swung toward him. "No, you aren't. I instructed you to come back to the car if they didn't have Abdul."

"They promised to return him," said Brent, his eyes sparking.

"People who break the law rarely keep their word," she blurted, immediately regretting her tone.

"So, you think they've already killed Abdul?"

"That's not what I'm saying. Kidnapping and plant poaching is one thing. Murder is another. There's a good chance Abdul is okay. I'm going to drop you off and go find him." She was surprised when Brent took her arm and pulled her to face him.

"I'm going with you," he said, his tone low, his face inches from hers.

Savannah knew Brent was acting out of concern for his colleague, but she couldn't help feeling a ping of excitement being this close to him. "You can let go of me now," she said, feeling his breath against her cheek.

"I need to be there. I won't take no for an answer."

"Fine. But you better listen this time." She didn't mean to sound so annoyed.

He let go of her arm, and she stepped back a couple of paces. Her arm burned where he had touched her, and she looked away.

"I'm sorry," he said after a moment. "This is a little new to me."

"It's okay, I get it. You're upset for your friend." She sent the man's face and cell phone number to Cherie, then scrolled through his text messages while she waited. It wasn't long before her phone rang.

"You got a location?" she asked Cherie.

"It's a burner, so still working on that, but we may not need it. The guy popped up in the database. Priors for armed robbery and assault. His family owns a piece of property not far from you. There's a barn."

"Send me the coordinates," said Savannah. Then she eyed the man on the ground. "Can you call the local PD to get this guy to the morgue?"

"Maybe you should ask them for backup?" suggested Cherie.

"We don't even know if they're at the property," said Savannah. "I'll do some recon first, so we'll be ready."

Cherie was silent on the other end of the phone.

"You there?" asked Savannah.

"There's a good chance Farran is already gone."

"I realize that." She looked out of the corner of her eye at Brent, whose expression was tense.

"Just be careful," said Cherie.

"Always."

As Savannah drove, she glanced at Brent, who stared straight ahead. "It's understandable if you want to sit this out," she said. "No one would blame you." Still no answer from him. "Brent, you okay?"

He turned in his seat to face her. "Can you tell me something?" he asked.

She glanced at him quickly, then pulled her attention back to the dark road. "What's the question?"

"What happened to your partner?"

Savannah's breath caught in her throat. She couldn't possibly tell him the truth about Jaime and her role in his death.

19

Savannah grappled for an answer to Brent's question when a truck sped up beside them and shots rang out, one crashing through the window.

"Get down!" she yelled as she began returning fire. After several shots, she must have hit the driver, because the truck swerved in front of them and went skidding across the road, careening over the right shoulder. She slammed on the brakes and pulled over. In the light of her headlights, she could see the truck flipped upside down in a ravine.

"We can't stop," said Brent, several cars pulling over as he spoke.

"Agreed," she said. "The kidnappers must know we got the guy they sent for the plants." She picked up her phone and made a call. "This is Agent Sanchez with the FBI. Can I speak to your chief?"

A man's voice came on the line. "Chief Sorenson. How can I help you?"

Savannah had to choose her words carefully. "A truck went into a ravine. If the driver is alive, he's wanted in connection with a federal case."

"Are you there now?"

"I need to leave the scene. I have an urgent matter to attend to in conjunction with the case."

"Okay, are you on Forrester Road? We just got a 911 call from there."

"Affirmative." Savannah hung up the phone and headed toward the barn where she hoped they'd find Abdul.

When they neared the property, Savannah's phone rang. A member of her team. "How far out are you?" she asked.

"Boss, we're snowed in. We can't get out of DC. They're saying it'll be at least twelve hours, maybe twenty-four."

"Keep me posted," she said and hung up without further comment. "My team is stuck in DC. We're on our own." She crept along the road until they came to the periphery of the property, then killed the engine and listened through the shattered window. The only sound was a dog barking somewhere in the distance.

Brent didn't speak until Savannah continued her thoughts. "We'll go in on foot and check the area. There are no lights, and I don't see a car. But we can't be certain there's no one around. Stay alert and be careful."

"I'll need a gun."

Savannah's brows shot up in surprise. "Have you ever shot a gun?"

"They trained us to shoot tranquilizer guns in case of animal attacks. You need to be precise to survive, so I think that counts."

"Just follow me closely. If shooting starts, press yourself to the ground behind something solid," she said.

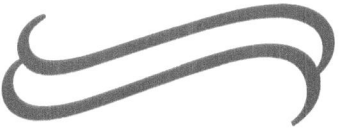

Brent wasn't about to steal across the property and enter the barn without a weapon. "I know you have more than one gun," he said, his voice firm.

"Fine," Savannah said, reaching in the back seat and unzipping a bag and removing a revolver. She handed it to him.

At the solid feel of the gun in his hands, relief washed through Brent. They climbed out of the car and closed their car doors quietly, then made their way down the edge of a long drive, staying in the shadows of the tall trees flanking the path. Before long, they came to a structure, its hulking frame reaching up into the dark sky. As they crept up to the side of the building, Brent listened intently. No sound from within. Savannah pressed her ear to the door, then wrapped her hand around the doorknob and turned. She pushed the door open slowly, and entered, Brent right behind her. Silence. After standing there for a moment, she pulled out her phone and turned on the light, sweeping the cavernous room for signs of life. The space was nothing but an empty shell that smelled as if hay had once been stored there. Savannah advanced into the room gun drawn, flashing the cell phone light onto a card table containing takeout containers. Brent touched the side of one. "Still warm," he said quietly.

"They must have been warned we were coming," Savannah said. She started to make a call, but Brent motioned for her to stop.

"I heard something," he whispered. "A scraping sound."

Savannah stood waiting.

Brent turned around. "Over there," he indicated the far wall with his head.

"Stay close," Savannah whispered as she made her way across the room toward the sound. When they were several yards away, she called out, "FBI. Is anyone there?"

There was a knocking sound in response.

Brent stayed with Savannah as they neared the far wall, where they found a door marked utility. She motioned for Brent to stand back, then trained her gun at the door and announced, "I'm armed and going to be opening the door." She reached forward and turned the knob. It was locked.

Brent glanced around the room for something heavy and spotted an array of tools on a nearby bench. He put the gun in the back of his pants and grabbed an ax. Savannah nodded an okay, and he smashed down on the doorknob several times until it loosened and hung there. Then he pulled open the door and stood back as Savannah trained the gun on the figure inside. It took Brent's eyes a moment to focus on the person huddled in the closet, his wrists bound and mouth covered in duct tape.

"Abdul!" cried Brent. He went into the closet and fell on his knees beside him. "Thank God you're okay."

Abdul's eyes suddenly widened in fear. A second later, a gunshot sounded and Brent felt a searing pain in his left arm. The utility closet door slammed shut, and more shots rang out.

His shirtsleeve quickly soaking with blood, Brent pulled the tape off Abdul's mouth with his good hand.

"Brent," Abdul said, his voice a low whisper. "You've been shot."

"I'm okay," he said, though he knew he had to stop the flow of blood running down his arm, or he'd soon be in trouble. He pulled off the bulletproof vest and removed his shirt, then took one arm of the shirt and with one hand looped it around his bicep just above the wound.

"Let me help," said Abdul, reaching with bound hands to assist Brent with pulling the sleeve tight around his arm and making a knot. When they'd finished, Brent tentatively felt below the gunshot wound, relieved to find the bleeding had already slowed considerably.

Brent strained to listen, but no sounds were coming from the room beyond. Had they shot Savannah? The thought they might have killed her clenched in his chest. He didn't hear more gunfire. He worked to quickly undo the knots on Abdul's wrists, then pulled the gun from his pants and whispered, "I'm going to crack the door. Prepare to make a run for it." Just then, he heard footsteps approach.

2 0

A rush of gratitude coursing through his veins at the sight of Savannah standing in the doorway, Brent tried to speak but the words didn't come out. His eyes blurry, she appeared little more than a black silhouette positioned there, golden hair cascading over her shoulders. He started to stand and found himself falling forward right before everything went dark.

When Brent came to, he heard sirens. A man leaned over him and tightened something on his arm.

"Savannah," Brent said, trying to make sense of what was happening. He felt a hand on his good arm, then her face came into view.

"I'm right here," she said. "We're taking you to the hospital. You lost a lot of blood, so stay still."

Brent closed his eyes as the sirens wailed in his ears.

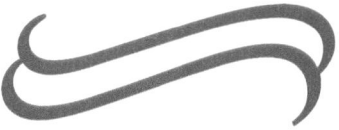

Savannah held onto Brent, watching as he struggled to stay conscious. "Is he going to be okay?" she asked the paramedic, worry mounting.

"Like you said, he's lost a lot of blood," the man said as he checked Brent's vitals. "The sooner we get him to the hospital, the better."

Five minutes later, they pulled in front of the hospital's emergency entrance. The paramedic driving hopped out and ran around to the back of the ambulance and pulled the doors open. Savannah climbed out quickly, then the two men lowered the gurney to the asphalt and sped toward the hospital doors. Savannah followed close behind as they wheeled the bed into the emergency room. When they got to the double doors of triage and told her to stay back, Savannah stopped and grabbed the wall to steady herself as Jaime's face right before he died flashed through her mind.

Two hours later after they had cauterized Brent's brachial artery to stop the bleeding, removed the bullet and stitched him up, Savannah was able to go and see him. She had pulled herself together, the confused tears she'd shed in the lady's room while they were stabilizing Brent now gone. She should never have let him come into the barn with her, and this was all going to stop. He would go home to recuperate under police surveillance while Savannah figured out what the hell was going on. Unfortunately, the storm in DC wasn't letting up, and her team still couldn't get here, but Savannah had worked alone many times before. Plastering a bright smile on her face, she clipped into Brent's room and announced, "You're looking much better than a couple of hours ago."

Brent raised up on one arm. "It's all a little blurry. The doctor said they removed a bullet from my arm. Where's Abdul?"

Savannah walked over to stand next to the bed. "You're all stitched up now. Abdul is home with his family. His injuries weren't as serious as yours. They treated him for some minor cuts and bruises and dehydration."

Brent tried to sit up. "He's still in danger and needs to be guarded. Can you do that?"

"Shh," said Savannah, "Lie back down and rest. I've got agents protecting him and his family until this case is closed. Your job is to rest and get better, okay?"

Brent lay back down then, his body relaxing into the mattress. He let out a sigh and before long fell asleep. Savannah sat down next to the bed and glanced at the monitor, noting that he seemed to be breathing easily and his heartbeat appeared steady. Though she should probably post a law enforcement officer in front of Brent's door and get back to the case before the trail ran cold on the kidnappers, something kept her here watching him instead. She checked her watch. Seven in the morning. A couple hours to catch her breath would be okay, she told herself. She laid her head back on the chair to rest for just a second.

It was late morning, bright sunlight filling the room, when Savannah heard her phone ringing. She sat upright, her eyes focusing on Brent, who was awake. Trying to push the grogginess away, she answered, "Sanchez."

"It's me, Cherie. You're in the hospital with Brent?"

At the urgency in Cherie's voice, Savannah woke up immediately. "Yes. What's going on?"

"We just got intel that several armed men are on their way to Brent's hospital room. I've notified local law enforcement, but they're five minutes out. You need to get out of there now."

Savannah slid her phone into her pocket and keeping her voice calm, said, "We need to leave ASAP. You able to walk?"

Brent slowly swung his legs to the edge of the bed and tried to stand. "Yes."

"Hold on," she said, unhooking the monitors. Then she grabbed their belongings. "Lean on me." She checked the hallway. No one in sight, so they started toward the exit. But after a few paces, the elevator doors opened, two men inside. She pulled Brent around and guided him the other direction, spotting a supply closet. The door was unlocked, so she yanked it open and waited for him to get inside, then followed, closing and locking the door behind her. They stood still for a few long moments as footsteps passed where they hid and kept going. Then Savannah shined her cell phone flashlight around the room. Spotting some scrubs on a top shelf, she grabbed them and pulled them on over her clothing, shoving her hair into a surgical cap. "They're not going to leave the hospital until they find us," she said. "Our best bet is to walk right past them. I know you're in pain but try not to let it show."

Brent nodded.

"Follow my lead," she said, then opened the door slowly, checking the hallway. Seeing the hall was empty, they slipped from the closet, then headed toward the main doors of the hospital entrance, Savannah steadying Brent's arm. "Don't look at anyone, no eye contact," she said as they emerged from the hallway to cross the main lobby.

The pain relievers the nurse gave Brent a couple of hours ago had done their job, but their effect was now slowing him down. As he shuffled next to Savannah in his hospital slippers, he kept his head down. At one point, two men walked by them quickly. Brent could tell by Savannah's stiffening posture that they were probably the men they were running from. When he and Savannah were just a few steps from leaving the building, a woman's voice called out, "Excuse me, can I ask where you're going?"

Savannah swung around and replied, "Official business." Then she headed them toward the sliding doors.

Brent would have given anything to lie down on a couch in the lobby. He called on every reserve in his body as they continued, hoping he wouldn't collapse. The pain was searing, but the effect of the medication was worse, his thinking impaired. Savannah guided him out the doors and onto the front walk. A woman drove up and got out of a Volvo, then ran around to help an older gentleman from the passenger side.

Savannah approached her and showed her badge. "I'm sorry, ma'am, but I will have to commandeer your vehicle. I know it's an inconvenience, but this is official business." The woman gaped at Savannah's outstretched hand. "Give me your keys, please."

The woman handed over her keys, calling after them as they got into the car. "When will I get my car back?"

"Soon," said Savannah, then barreled out of the hospital parking lot, melding into the traffic.

21

After they had driven for a couple of minutes, Savannah pulled her phone out of her pocket and dialed a number as she drove. "We're out," she said, listening for a moment. "Alright. I need you to send me coordinates for the nearest safe house." She paused, then and glanced at Brent. "He's doing okay. They removed the bullet and stitched him up before we had to leave."

When she hung up the phone, she held it aloft with one hand, until a text came in. She tapped on the phone and a map sprang onto the screen. "Would you mind keeping an eye on this and telling me which way to go?" she asked Brent.

He took the phone and watched as a red dot made its way west. "I've never been to a safe house before. How's it different?"

Savannah let out a short laugh. "They're nothing to write your mama about, as my gramma would say. But they do the trick. Hidden away and secure."

"As in keeping us hidden from the world?" said Brent, visions of the last several hours flashing through his mind.

They passed a river and entered a more deserted part of the terrain.

Savannah drove around a tree limb in the road. "Yes, it'll give us somewhere to lie low for a while so you can catch your breath. Hopefully it's a nice, quiet place."

A half hour later, they headed down a road lined with towering trees and thick, green vegetation. Brent could smell pine and camphor. When the arrow on the screen indicated they'd arrived, he told Savannah to make a right down a long drive that passed through dense shrubbery. She stopped in front of a little wooden house set up against the woods. He handed her the phone.

Savannah glanced at the screen. "Thanks for navigating. I'm glad we're here so you can get a chance to sleep and heal. I would love a little downtime myself." She smiled.

They got out of the car and Savannah pulled off the scrubs, throwing them in the back seat. Then she grabbed their things, and they walked on the spongy ground, littered with layers of pine needles. When they arrived at the front door, Savannah checked the texted instructions, then told him, "Wait a moment while I get the key." She went around the back of the house and returned to open the screen door and slid a key into the lock. Over her shoulder, she said, "Keep an eye out here, and I'll check the house."

Brent watched her go inside, trying to wrap his head around how his life had taken such a sinister turn. A tightness filled his chest when he thought of Abdul's close call, and he let out one long breath. One thing he wouldn't change, though, was meeting Savannah.

She returned a minute later. "It's not bad for a safe house," she said. "Come on in."

Brent entered and glanced around. The place was small,

like his cabin. The front area had a kitchen with a compact, round table, and a living room with windows covered in partially open blinds. He could see the green of woods through the slats.

Savannah checked the locks and set the heat. "There's a bedroom at the end of the hall. Feel free to go take a nap."

Brent nodded and headed down the short hallway, suddenly feeling overwhelmed by fatigue. There was one room with an adjoining bathroom. He sat on the side of the bed and thought about changing out of the hospital gown and into his clothing, but they were probably bloodstained, and he was too tired, anyway. Instead, he pulled back the covers and got in bed, soon finding himself drifting into a hazy sleep.

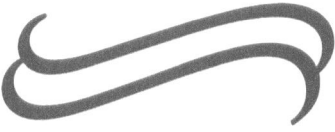

Savannah surveyed the fuel situation and contents of the refrigerator and cupboards. The generator was full, so they would be okay for a while. Enough food to keep them fed—granola, heaps of canned soup, coffee, and frozen meals in the freezer. Now she just had to figure out what the hell was going on. She sat down at the kitchen table and ran through the last few days. What was the common denominator? The orchids, obviously, and then Macintosh. But how could he be alive? She had watched Jaime put a bullet in his chest.

She glanced down the hallway, then got up from the table and headed to the bedroom, trying to walk as quietly as possible. When she got to the doorway and saw Brent splayed out on the bed, she wasn't sure at first if he was asleep, but then she noticed his chest rising and falling in a steady rhythm. She went to the foot of the bed and gazed down at him in the stillness. As she watched his handsome, peaceful face, she had to admit to herself there was more going on here than just the case. Something she hadn't felt in half a decade. She wasn't sure where it would go from here, but she felt both excited and frightened to have suddenly come out of what had felt like a dead sleep of despair.

It was early evening and Savannah was mapping out the case on a piece of paper, drawing lines between who was involved and with what and whom, hoping to see a pattern. She was intently studying the chart when she heard movement from the bedroom. Standing quickly and grabbing her gun, she went down the hall to find Brent awake. His eyes went to the gun and widened.

"Sorry," she said, setting the weapon on a nearby dresser. "You've probably seen your share of firearms for one day. Just making sure you're safe. Feeling any better?"

"I am. I slept really well," he said, making an effort to get up.

Savannah approached with her palm out. "Before you get out of bed, let me check your wound first. Make sure the stitches are still intact."

"Go ahead, nurse. I'm in your care." He laughed.

Savannah leaned over Brent and began gently pulling up on the hospital gown.

"Let me make it easier for you." He sat up and reached with his good arm to pull the gown off himself, then lay back down.

At the sight of his broad chest, excitement raced through Savannah. She tried to focus on the wound and nodded in approval. "The bandage is still intact. Let me take a peek underneath." She reached over and turned on the bedside light, then leaned in close and gently lifted the edge of the bandage, her heart pounding the closer she got to Brent. What was he thinking? She wondered, her emotions like a rubber band stretched to the limit.

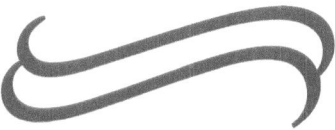

When Savannah leaned over him, her long, silken hair touched Brent's bare chest and sent sizzles throughout him. He felt the urge to kiss her and thought how insane that was. She'd been a little flirty occasionally, although maybe he'd imagined it. Mostly, Savannah had stayed focused on her job and why they were here. Still, he couldn't deny his attraction to her.

Savannah stayed near for a moment, then pulled away and met his gaze. "I'm not seeing a lot of red that would indicate infection." She remained close, her eyes on his, the invisible strings between them taut.

22

"You're a beautiful woman," said Brent, his voice deep, serious. He had meant to keep his emotions under control, but the words had slipped out. He waited, his eyes locked on hers.

Savannah remained still. "It's been a long time since a man told me that."

Brent searched her face. "Your lips, they look so soft," he said out loud, trying to stop the words falling from his mouth. I'm acting like a fool, he thought, but he couldn't stop himself. "Has it been a long time since a man kissed you?" he asked, almost in a whisper. He longed to murmur the words into her hair, smell the scent of her.

From what Brent had seen, shyness wasn't one of Savannah's attributes, but she remained quiet, a faint blush covering her cheeks.

"What if I kiss you?" he said, his heart hammering.

"I wouldn't stop you, if that's what you're asking."

Brent smiled and reached for her, pulling her to him and taking her lips in his. The sweetness of the moment washed through him like a shot of warm liqueur, something to savor as he became intoxicated in the wonder of Savannah. He could feel their hearts synchronized as they pressed against one another. The kiss aroused and inflamed him. He explored her lips again and again, then trailed his tongue down the side of her neck, feeling her tremble as he kissed the soft, pale curve of her skin. It had been so long since he had held and made love to a woman. "Take your clothes off," he breathed in her ear.

Savannah smiled and stood next to the bed, shimmying out of her pants and panties and slowly unbuttoning her blouse. Then she reached around and unclasped her bra to reveal her round, full breasts, the nipples taut. He felt like a man starved for beauty and couldn't take his eyes off her pale pink, almost pearlescent body. He rose from the bed suddenly, surprising her by sweeping her off her feet and lowering her gently onto the duvet. She lay her head back as Brent caressed her breasts and took them in his hands to kiss their silky softness, taste them. The steamy desire between the two of them was more than Brent could have imagined. He slowly and deliberately touched her every curve and pleasure point, rubbed her buttocks, nipples, her inner thighs, and back. Kissed the softness between her legs and slipped his tongue inside her until she gasped and sat up to take his erection in both her hands. He groaned as she caressed him until he stopped her. Then she lay back and opened her legs, and Brent eased down, powerful and slow, until he was fully inside her, moving with a deliberate rhythm meant to make her happy.

"Make love to me, Brent," she whispered at last, digging her nails into his back. As he continued, she cried, "Don't stop, don't stop."

Savannah had almost forgotten the strength of a man's arms, the smell of fresh male sweat. She had been protecting Brent, but now she was the one who felt safe in his arms. She had no idea how things had gotten this far but she knew there was nothing she wanted more.

It wasn't until after they had loved one another for several hours that she remembered his wound. She turned toward him and lay a hand on his chest.

"I'm sorry. Did I hurt you?"

His face relaxed, Brent answered, "If you did, I wouldn't know. That was incredible."

His words made her feel good, but also uncomfortable. "I'm going to go check and make sure no one tried to break the door down," she said, slipping out of the bed.

"As if we would have heard it." He stretched his naked body, enticing her into the bed.

Savannah eyed the spot next to Brent and thought about lying back down next to him but needed to clear her head and focus. She slid her underwear and pants back on, then grabbed her bra and shirt and padded down the hall. Once back in the living room, she stood in the dark, trying to get her wits about her. Making love with a man had never felt like this. She smiled, remembering the intensity, the words of tenderness he spoke to her. What was she doing? She groaned. She was supposed to be working. Jaime came to her then. What would he have thought about her actions? She looked at the evidence map on the table, then glanced down the hallway. Brent was still in the bedroom. Thinking what? That she had run out of the room like a coward?

Ten minutes later, Brent emerged from the bedroom, a pair of sweats and a T-shirt on. "I found these in the dresser in there," he said. "I hope it's okay to wear them."

Savannah glanced up as he entered, then went back to examining her map. "That's what the clothing is for," she said.

"What's that?" he asked, coming to stand by her chair.

"I call it an evidence map."

"So, you really do like maps. Does it help?" He sat down next to her.

"A lot of times, it does."

"This time?"

Savannah pointed to a name in the center of the page that said Macintosh. "This man is supposed to be dead. As a matter of fact, I saw him shot in the chest. He couldn't still be alive, but his name keeps coming up." Savannah appeared reflective for a moment, then she spoke. "About what happened in there. I..." she trailed off.

"You what?" asked Brent.

Savannah kept her eyes on the map as Brent waited for her reply. "It's just," she glanced up, then back down. "It's been a long time."

"You didn't seem rusty," he offered.

"That's not what I meant. It's just that the last time I was with someone, I was—"

"With your husband," Brent cut her off. "So, this was what, a blip?"

Savannah could hear what sounded like disappointment seeping into Brent's tone. She didn't want that. "No, it wasn't a blip."

He leaned closer to her, and she could feel his eyes on her, but still, she didn't look at him. "What was it?" he asked. "I was involved, so it'd be good for me to know."

JULIE BAWDEN DAVIS

She looked over at him feeling terrible. "It was beautiful, but I..."

Brent sighed. "Never mind. This is clearly not a comfortable conversation for you. I don't want to push."

Savannah saw hurt lining his face. How could she explain herself? She was struggling to form an explanation that might make sense when her phone buzzed.

"You better get it," he said.

She nodded and grabbed the phone. It was Cherie.

"The team is still stuck here, boss, but I have some info. Someone matching Macintosh's description was spotted by the Los Angeles Port Authority getting off a cruise ship last week. It was originally flagged but then dismissed when he showed up as deceased in the system."

"What was the origin of the ship?"

"Tokyo. I was thinking about the yen left in your car."

Savannah sat there for a moment as the information sank in. "Do you think it really was him?"

Cherie was silent on the other end of the phone for a few beats. "That night went sideways in more ways than one," she said softly. "They never did identify all the body parts after the blast. I'd say anything is possible."

23

When Savannah hung up, Brent said, "That sounded serious."

She tapped her pen on the evidence map. "It was."

When she didn't offer any more information, he got a glass out of the cupboard and filled it with water, then took a long drink. He turned around and leaned against the counter, watching her examine her map. What was she thinking, he wondered? That she regretted their getting together? It had felt so real and right, he couldn't believe that was the case.

"There's food in the fridge if you want anything," said Savannah, who had started writing on her map again.

Brent pulled open the refrigerator, then the freezer, spying some frozen meals. "Want anything?"

"I'm not really hungry but thank you."

Brent yanked a chicken dinner out of its carton and put it in the microwave. While it heated up, he thought about his sister, who he usually talked to every couple of days. His phone had been off, so she was probably starting to worry.

Savannah looked over at him. "How's your shoulder?"

"Healing," said Brent, taking his meal to the table and

sitting down. He stirred the mashed potatoes. "I'm curious about something."

She set down her pen. "What's that?"

"How do you do your job and manage a family? I mean, I know you don't have children, but you have people you love, like your sister and nephew."

Savannah sighed. "To be honest, it's not easy. There are cases that have me underground like we are now for weeks on end. My sister and brother-in-law are used to it, but my nephew doesn't always understand. I've missed a few important occasions, and there was no way to explain those absences in a way that made sense to him. I just try to be as present as possible when I'm with them. And to let them know I love them, so that if something ever does happen...." She trailed off.

"That's the best thing to do, no matter your profession," said Brent. "I try to do that with my sister. Not that forest work is that dangerous, although there's this. I really should contact her. She's going to be worried."

"Okay, you can use my phone, but don't give anything away. We don't want to put her in danger."

Brent nodded and dialed Becky's number. He waited to hear her voice on the other end of the line admonishing him for not calling sooner, but it went straight to voicemail. He hung up. "No answer," he said. "She must still be at yoga class."

Savannah watched Brent clean up after his dinner and go to the back of the house and heard him turn on the shower.

A part of her wanted to join him. To press away the reality of now and enjoy him. But she needed to stay clearheaded so she could figure out their next moves. They couldn't stay here indefinitely. She looked up the weather in D.C. and saw that the storm raged on. Then she got up and checked the locks on the windows and doors, shutting off all but one small light. Once it sounded like Brent had gone to sleep, she went into the bathroom and took a quick shower. After toweling off, she walked softly into the bedroom and quietly opened dresser drawers until she found some fresh clothing. She pulled a man's oversized T-shirt over her head and it ran past her knees. Then she turned to the bed and the empty space beside Brent. It would be so easy and comfortable to climb in next to him. She yearned to feel the heat of his body warming hers. But would that be fair to him? She felt a jumble of emotions—most of which she couldn't identify.

She went back to the living room where she moved her gun to the coffee table, then lay down on the couch. There she stared at the ceiling for some time as milky light from the moon filtered into the room, creating shadows. Finally, she drifted into a fitful sleep.

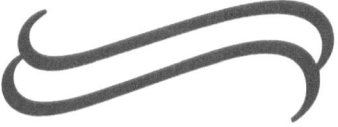

Brent awoke in the morning to the smell of coffee. He yawned and stretched, then sat up to check his bandage. The wound looked like it was really healing.

Just then Savannah walked in, dressed in a man's shirt, her long hair cascading over her shoulders. He was glad to be under the covers, so she couldn't see how the sight of her immediately aroused him. "The coffee smells good," he said, trying to keep his tone even.

"I can get you some, if you like." She pulled open drawers and began taking out clothing and holding it up. When she found a white tailored blouse and black pants and some women's underwear, she put the clothing under her arm and turned to face him. She appeared as if she might say something, then seemed to change her mind and headed to the bathroom. "Feel free to get another change of clothing," she said before closing the door.

Brent heard the water turn on, so he got up and began rummaging in the drawers to find something to wear. Most of the clothing was too small, but he finally found a pair of tan pants and a blue striped shirt. He pulled off what he was wearing and was reaching for the clean shirt when Savannah walked out of the bathroom, her eyes flying up and down his body.

"Sorry," he said. "I thought you'd be in the bathroom longer." He stood there, unmoving. When she also stayed put, he shrugged and pulled on the underwear and pants. He was about to put on the shirt when Savannah cleared her throat. He waited again, as she seemed to be waging a private battle. Then he kept dressing. "This is obviously uncomfortable for you. Let's just forget about what happened," he said. "Chalk it off to a heat-of-the-moment moment."

Savannah's eyes glistened with what looked like pain, and he felt a ping in his chest. He went over to her. "It's obvious you're holding onto something," he said in a low voice. "I'm here if you want to talk about it."

Savannah nodded, her eyes bright. "I'm sure that would help, but I just don't know how."

24

Brent moved closer, then said, "You start with one word and then that leads to the next word. You want to stop talking, you stop talking."

Savannah nodded. "I can give it a shot."

"How about we get some coffee first?" he suggested.

After they had settled down at the kitchen table, each with a full mug of coffee, Savannah shifted in her chair, then started. "Jaime and I met my first day out of Quantico. He was older than me by several years. He had a certain charisma that commanded center stage whenever he walked into a room." She looked up at Brent, then back down at her coffee and took a sip.

"It was a couple of years later that I left the CSI lab to go out on my first field assignment. The supervisor paired me with Jaime. Figured he could teach me the ropes better than anyone. And he did. I learned a great deal under his watch. So much so that I rose in rank during the three years we worked together."

Savannah stopped then and put a lump of sugar in her coffee, stirring it and setting down the spoon. "It was pretty obvious to both of us that we had feelings for each other. We tried to hold back, but everything came to a head one night when we were on a stakeout. We'd been working together for nearly three years by then. When we decided to get married and he moved to another division, we were warned about how us both being in the Bureau was going to be difficult. But it seemed to work out. For a while." Savannah glanced outside at the day, which was bright and cold. Then she checked her cell phone.

"You said, for a while," said Brent.

Savannah nodded. "Jaime was..." She stopped. "He needed constant stimulation. I didn't realize until we had been married for a couple of months that he was addicted to adrenaline. It was always more and more risk and less and less wiggle room. I knew he was in trouble with the last case he was on. He was on edge all the time, even when he was supposed to be sleeping. I'd find him standing in the living room checking out the windows. I loved him, I did, but those last few months, it was as if he changed. He became more and more driven. At all costs."

Savannah looked as if she might cry. She brushed the back of her hand across her eyes and took a gulp of coffee. "I got angry and accused him of loving the job more than me. Even as I said the things I said, I realized I was falling into the trap that everyone had warned us about."

Brent grabbed a napkin and handed it to her. She dabbed the tears forming at the corners of her eyes, then resumed. "One night, he told me they were closing in on a suspect. The man was into high stakes art and antiquities theft. He'd stolen valuable pieces from some of the most renowned museums in the world. But he was elusive and had been evading the Bureau for years. Even worse, taunting us. Jaime became rabid about catching the guy. The suspect was William Macintosh."

She picked up the sugar bowl and set it back down again. "Something odd happened when Jaime told me about Macintosh. I don't know if it was envy on my part that I wasn't involved in terms of my career, or if it was just because I missed what we had, but I wanted to be there when Jaime brought Macintosh down. So, when he left that night, I followed him. I figured I'd just tail him and watch from afar. What harm could I do?" Savannah took another sip of coffee and shifted in her chair.

"Things quickly went sideways. Macintosh was having Jaime watched, so when I followed him, they were tailing me. Several armed men surrounded my car and forced me out, then brought me into Jaime's meeting with Macintosh, who thought he was meeting a stolen arts dealer. Macintosh's men drew their guns on Jaime, demanding to know if he was working with the feds. When he denied it, Macintosh told Jamie he should have no problem with Macintosh killing me and dumping my body in the Potomac. When Macintosh went to fire his gun at me, Jaime got a shot off first, hitting him in the chest. All of Macintosh's men responded by shooting Jaime."

Savannah gulped back a sob as Brent put his hand on hers. "I took advantage of the chaos and ran like I knew Jaime would have wanted me to. I left him there. It turns out I got out of there just in time. I was a block away when the building blew up."

Brent got up and went around to the other side of the table and pulled Savannah out of the chair and into his arms as she sobbed. When the tears finally subsided, he rubbed a hand gently along her back. "Jaime wouldn't want you to carry this guilt around anymore. You said it yourself, he did what he did so you could live."

With Brent's steady arms soothing her, Savannah felt as if a barrier had been lifted in some way. She pulled back and looked into his face. "Thank you," she said quietly, her arms tight around him.

"I can't imagine what you went through," he said, his voice soft.

"I survived," she said.

"You did."

"But now..." she started, unsure of exactly what she wanted to say.

Brent raised his eyebrows. "But now?"

"I feel like..." Savannah struggled to put into words, what? That she thought there was something between her and Brent? That she wanted to continue and see where it went? Why couldn't she just spit it out? Just then, her phone rang, jolting her back to reality. She pulled from his arms and checked the screen. "Sorry, I have to get this. Cherie, what's the word?"

"The team is still here, but I have some information about Brent's sister, Becky Larson. I've been monitoring her, as you asked."

Savannah shot a look at Brent, whose back was turned as he poured himself another cup of coffee. "Yeah?"

"Word just came in from LAPD that she was abducted from her apartment last night. An eyewitness saw two armed men take her."

25

"Dammit," she said as Brent turned to eye her. "Is there any surveillance footage?"

"Apparently not."

"Send me anything you can dig up." Savannah hung up the phone and faced Brent, who had set down his coffee, his arms on the back of a chair.

"Is it Abdul?" he asked.

Savannah took a deep breath and gestured to the chair. "You might want to sit down."

Brent's eyes widened. "Just tell me."

"It's your sister. She was taken from her apartment last night."

"What the hell are you talking about?" Brent's hands grasped the chair hard. "Who told you she was taken?" He grabbed his phone from the table and turned it on, then pressed a number and waited. Raw fear covered his face. He slammed the phone down. "Who took her? And what about Russ?"

"That's the boyfriend, right? He wasn't on the scene when

the local PD arrived. Look, this could just be a misunderstanding," she said, trying to calm him down.

"A misunderstanding?" Brent's face had become bright red.

"We'll figure this out," she said.

Brent shoved his phone into his pocket. "I'm going to Los Angeles right now to find my sister."

Savannah approached Brent. "Hold on. There are men after us."

"I don't care. I am not sitting here on my hands while who knows what happens to my sister." The terror on his face was palpable as he uttered his last words.

Savannah put her hands on his arms and said in a steady voice, "I'm not asking you to sit on your hands. We just need to think this through carefully before we make any moves."

Brent's expression became stony. "I am going to LA today. I'm bringing the orchids with me. You want to stop me; you'll have to shoot me."

Savannah gave him a small smile. "I think you've been shot enough for now. I'll make the arrangements for us to fly out later today. Now can you sit down for a minute while I do that?"

Relief flooded Brent's face. He nodded and pulled out a chair while Savannah checked her texts. Good. Contact information for a detective at the LAPD. She dialed his number and a gravelly voice soon came on the line.

"Detective Caruso, this is Savannah Sanchez with the FBI, I understand you caught a case last night. Abducted female, Becky Larson."

"That's right, Agent Sanchez. Not much to report yet. We're still canvassing the area. An eyewitness saw her pulled from her apartment but wasn't able to give us much else. I'll keep you posted."

"There is someone who lives with her. Russ Parker. Any sign of him?"

She heard paper rustling on the other end of the phone. "A neighbor did inform us that she lives with a boyfriend. We haven't located him yet."

"I might have his cell phone number," she said, getting Brent's attention. "Russ's number?"

Brent nodded and checked his phone, then gave her the number.

"I believe this is related to a case of mine involving the poaching of rare orchids," Savannah said. "I'm going to fly in today."

"You telling me you're taking jurisdiction over this case?"

"I'm not concerned with jurisdiction at this point," said Savannah. "We need all the help we can get to find this woman. The man who likely has her is extremely dangerous."

"You've got a suspect?"

"William Macintosh."

The man didn't speak for a moment. "Wasn't he killed a few years back?"

"That was the thought but it looks like he is still at large."

"Well, that changes everything," said Caruso. "I'll increase manpower on my end. It will take both our agencies to bring a man like Macintosh in, and I'll be happy to do it. Give me a call when you land. I'll have a car come pick you up."

Savannah hung up the phone to meet Brent's shocked face. "You think William Macintosh has my sister?"

Savannah swallowed. "Reports have a man fitting his description getting off a ship in LA a few days ago."

Brent jumped up, the chair clattering across the floor. "And you didn't bother to tell me?"

"I'm sorry. This thing has been unraveling fast. We'll find your sister. I promise. Let me find us the quickest way out of here."

Brent regretted not warning his sister when all of this started. But Savannah was right. Things had escalated quickly. A week ago, his life was predictable. He and his sister usually talked several times a week. She'd often forget the time difference between them and call and wake him up late at night. Brent would shake himself out of sleep and listen to one of her animated, long stories about eating dinner in the same restaurant as a celebrity or working out next to a movie producer. He could tell she missed their parents, and she needed to talk. Truth was, he needed to talk on those nights as much as she did.

26

After making several phone calls, Savannah arranged for them to get a flight out on a private jet that night. When it was time to leave the safe house, she handed Brent the keys and said, "You can drive. I'll navigate." She tried to catch his eye, but he headed straight out and was soon in the car behind the wheel. Savannah shut the door to the safe house and hid the key in the back, then got in the passenger seat. "You'll want to head east at the end of the drive," she told him.

After a few minutes, Brent finally spoke, "I heard you on the phone. You're going to do private security for someone in exchange for this flight?"

Savannah checked their destination on her cell phone. "Yeah, I do that sometimes. The daughter of the man who owns the plane is having her bachelorette party in Martinique next month. Take the 15 south up here." She pointed.

"We're flying on a private plane?"

"If we flew commercial, we wouldn't be there until who knows when tomorrow. And despite what you see on TV, the

Bureau doesn't have planes ready and waiting when we're on a case."

Brent sped up to merge onto the 15. "Thank you for getting us to LA so quickly."

"It's my job," Savannah replied. As soon as she said it, she regretted it. Why couldn't she tell Brent the truth? That she cared about him and anyone close to him?

When they arrived at the airfield, it was just past midnight. Brent drove into the hangar and parked, then shut off the engine. Cherie had arranged for someone to return the vehicle to its owner, along with some cash to compensate them. The steward welcomed them when they boarded and asked if they'd like a drink. Savannah ordered a vodka tonic, while Brent asked for a beer.

As they made themselves comfortable on the plush, leather seats, Savannah thought how ordinarily she would have enjoyed traveling in style, but now she could only focus on finding Brent's sister before something happened to her. She thought about Macintosh, whose MO had always been transporting contraband. If Becky's disappearance was his doing, it would be his first abduction. She remembered Jaime once telling her the man he was after was unpredictable and thrived on the chase.

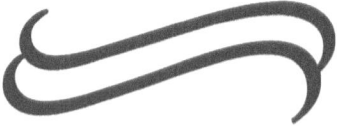

Brent thanked the steward for the beer and took several sips, willing himself to calm down. They would be in LA in a few hours. Savannah sat across from him. She took a sip of her drink, then gave him a tentative smile.

"Sorry about losing it earlier back at the safe house," he said.

Savannah sat up and set her drink in the armrest. "No need to apologize. Family is family. I get it."

Brent glanced out at the dark sky as the plane began taxiing for takeoff. He asked the question he'd been afraid to ask. "Do you think my sister is still alive?"

"I think she is," Savannah said in the no-nonsense tone he'd come to know well. "If they wanted her dead, she'd be dead. They have her because they want something. The orchids."

Brent nodded, knowing that Savannah's logic played out. He glanced at the plants in the plastic case. Who would have ever imagined that the orchids he had walked by so many times would become a bargaining chip for his sister?

After finishing his beer, he put his head back on the seat. Listening to the drone of the airplane engine, he soon found himself drifting off to sleep. He dreamed vivid, lucid dreams. His sister was with him, insisting that he take off his bandage so she could see his wound. She kept talking about how Mom and Dad would be mad that he had gotten shot. Then a raven flew by, squawking, and his sister started to fade away.

The plane set down at the Santa Monica Airport at nearly five am. Savannah, who had stayed awake during the flight watching Brent sleep and trying to figure out next steps, shook his shoulder gently. "We're here," she said.

He opened his eyes and sat up quickly. "LA?"

"Santa Monica," she said. "Not far from the LAPD. We're meeting my contact there." She stood and stretched.

"Did you get any sleep?" he asked as they disembarked.

"A little." She lied.

Outside in the still dark morning, the scent of jet fuel in the air, she pulled out her phone and dialed Caruso's number. "You here?" he asked.

"Affirmative."

"I'll have a car there within fifteen minutes. I have some potential good news waiting."

Savannah hung up the phone and said, "Someone will be here shortly." She thought about telling Brent there was good news but decided against it. A police officer's idea of good news could be quite different than that of a civilian's.

27

When they arrived at LAPD headquarters, the sky had started to lighten. Brent looked up at a multi-story glass building glinting in the sun.

"This is nicer than the Bureau's headquarters," Savannah commented as they headed down a walkway toward the front of the building.

Before long, a man exited the doors and approached them. He had salt-and-pepper, close-cropped hair and was compact and muscular. His gun holster stood out against his white dress shirt. He walked at a brisk pace and soon extended his hand in greeting to Savannah. "You must be Agent Sanchez. Max Caruso."

"Nice to meet you," she said, motioning to Brent. "This is Brent Larson. The victim's brother." At her choice of words, Brent tensed.

Max turned to Brent and shook his hand. "We've got some potential good news about your sister's whereabouts. Let's head inside, and I'll fill you in." He turned back toward the building as Savannah and Brent followed.

As they waited for the elevator, Caruso said, "I work in

major crimes, but we're partnering with white collar on this, since it's suspected that Macintosh is involved." The elevator doors opened and he gestured them inside.

When they got out on the fifth floor, Caruso led them to a conference room where two men sat sorting through papers at an oval table.

"This is Detective Dorsett and Detective Song," he said of the two men. "Meet Agent Savannah Sanchez from the FBI and Brent Larson, brother of Becky Larson." He motioned to a table against the far wall. "There's coffee if you want."

Savannah headed to the coffee pot as Brent pulled out a chair. "I'd rather hear your good news about my sister's whereabouts," he said.

Detective Caruso sat down and took a slug of coffee from a cup sitting on the table. "Dorsett and Song have been monitoring the financial movements of a local Japanese expat named Akira Nagaya, who has some properties here. They've suspected him of smuggling stolen collectables for some time. Your comment about poached plants caught my attention. The detectives have found some deposits to an account in the Cayman Islands. Turns out the Islands' Department of Environment has seen a dramatic increase in plant poaching in recent months. They have some of the rarest plants in the world there."

"You're thinking they're holding Becky Larson on one of his properties?" asked Savannah.

"It's possible."

"How many properties are there?"

"Three, but we've already checked one downtown, and it's empty. That leaves a mansion in Pacific Palisades, and a remote location in Calabasas. My bet is on the remote location. Easier to fly under the radar out there."

"If they've got a lot of sensitive, rare plants, they would want to be near the humidity of the ocean," said Brent.

"Greenhouses wouldn't be enough in Calabasas. It's too dry. I've been there."

Caruso looked at Savannah. "Your call. It's a thirty-minute drive to Calabasas."

Though Brent had a point about the plants, Savannah agreed with Caruso. The remote location would be a much safer place to stash rare goods and Becky. "Let's go to Calabasas," she said finally.

"You're going to have to stay here," said Caruso to Brent.

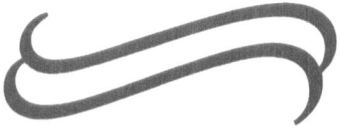

Brent watched everyone leave, anger swelling inside of him. While he understood Savannah's choice, the fact that she didn't seem to consider what he had to say about the plants angered him. This was his sister's life.

He glanced at the table where one of the detectives had left a file folder. He reached for it and began shuffling through the papers until he found what he was looking for. An address in Pacific Palisades. He grabbed a pen on the table and wrote the address on the inside flap of his shirt, then put the paper back in the file. As he did so, the doorknob to the room turned. He took several long strides to the coffee machine and picked the carafe up, then swung around.

"Excuse me," said the detective named Song. He picked up the file folder and left.

Brent put down the carafe and went to the doorway, opening it a crack and checking the hallway. Then he picked up the case of orchids and left the room, making his way to the elevator. When he got to the bottom floor, he waited until the woman at the front desk was busy signing in a

visitor and slipped out the front door. As he walked toward the street, Brent wondered how he was going to get to Pacific Palisades. He'd been in LA a few times before and knew that taxis were hard to find. He didn't want to turn on his phone to get a ride, in case the men who had been following them in North Carolina were tracking him. As he stood there, the orchid box tucked under his arm, a twenty-something couple, both holding paper coffee cups, walked up. The woman peered at the case and exclaimed, "Those are gorgeous. Are they orchids?"

"They are," said Brent. "I'm supposed to deliver them to someone in Pacific Palisades. But my phone is dead, so I can't order an Uber. If I were to give you some cash, could you order me one?"

The girl glanced at her boyfriend, who shrugged his shoulders. Five minutes later, Brent was headed to Pacific Palisades.

As they drove to the remote location, Caruso at the wheel, Savannah thought about what Brent had said about the plants. Could he have been right? If Nagaya was as fanatical as he seemed, maybe he was keeping them near the beach. In that case, they were heading away from Becky Larson, whose time was quickly running out.

28

Brent had the driver drop him a few houses away from Nagaya's. The man likely had surveillance, and Brent didn't want to be on camera until he was ready.

He crouched on the side of the street and opened the case of orchids. They were holding up. Looking around, he spotted some thick shrubbery, then went over, and, trying to be as inconspicuous as possible, put the box underneath out of the sun. Then he headed to the tall wrought iron gate in front of Nagaya's home. As suspected, a camera pointed down on him from the top of the gate. He pushed a button and waited. Seconds later, a woman's voice came on the line. "Who is there?"

Brent cleared his throat. "Brent Larson. I'm here to discuss a transaction with Mr. Nagaya regarding rare orchids."

Moments later, the gate squeaked on its hinges as it slid open. Brent walked through and headed down a pathway lined with rare cycads. Normally, he would stop to admire such horticultural gems, but all he could think about was Becky. Before long, the path widened and ended at a low-slung building with floor to ceiling windows positioned to take advantage of the surrounding vegetation. A Bentley was parked in the drive. He walked to the front door as it opened. A small, wizened woman stood on the threshold.

"Mrs. Nagaya?" he asked.

She shook her head. "I am Mr. Nagaya's housekeeper." She stepped back. "Please, come in."

Brent walked into a foyer lit by the sunshine coming in from the windows. Surrounding him were ornate pieces of art. Sculptures and vases sat in alcoves, and paintings lined the walls.

"You will find Mr. Nagaya in the conservatory," she said, pointing to a hallway.

Brent headed that way, soon coming to a room with a massive domed ceiling made of colored, refracted glass. The effect was a kaleidoscope of light. The room was lined with towering palms draped with vining philodendron, and orchids hung suspended from the greenery. A giant fountain covered one wall, the sound of trickling water echoing in the space. He walked over to see jewel-colored koi swimming in a pool at the base of the fountain. Suspended from above were strands of Spanish moss interlaced with yellow and white orchids.

"I see you admire the Fuukiran orchids," said a man's voice, causing Brent to swing around to face him. "They have been grown for 300 years and were originally collected from the wild to be given to the Shogun to gain political favor. They are only fragrant at night."

The man wore black pants and a black shirt with a red, silk handkerchief in the pocket. He smiled and bowed slightly. "You have asked to see me, Mr. Larson. I am Akira Nagaya. How may I help you?"

"I've come to make a trade," said Brent.

The man raised an eyebrow. "And what would you have to trade?"

Brent paused for a nanosecond. "I have the rare orchids you want. Just give me my sister."

The man eyed Brent for a moment, then said, "I'm afraid I know nothing of your sister. She is lost?"

Brent quelled the anger building in his chest. "I have reason to believe she is here. I have the orchids from the forest in North Carolina. You give me Becky, I give you the orchids."

"You seem to be upset about your sister, which I can certainly understand, but I'm not able to help you with that."

Brent wasn't leaving without his sister. "Enough games, Nagaya. Give me Becky, and I'll be on my way."

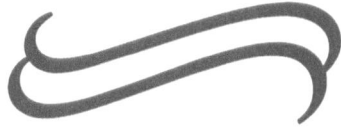

Caruso slowed the car as they approached the Calabasas location. "How do you want to do this?" he asked.

"Do you have a heat signature tracker?" asked Savannah.

He pulled one out of the glove compartment and handed it to Savannah. Then he parked, and she got out of the car and aimed it at the building several yards in from the road.

"I'm getting one signature," said Savannah. "The person seems to be moving back and forth, maybe working on something." She handed the tracker back to Caruso. "I'm going to knock on the door and play lost. Back me up."

She headed down the dusty driveway toward an industrial building. When she got to the front door, which displayed the words Nagaya Industries, she rapped several times, then stepped back, ready to pull her gun if needed.

The door opened slowly, and a young Asian man peeked out. "Can I help you?"

The man's voice stopped Savannah for a second. It sounded familiar. "I'm not from here, and I seem to have lost my way," she said. "I was hoping you could give me some directions." Savannah tried to peer behind the man, but he held the door tight.

"Where are you trying to go?" he said, his eyes wary.

That voice again, thought Savannah. "I'm trying to get to my aunt's house. She lives up the road."

The man appeared to be formulating a response when it hit her. "You gave me the orchid photos!" she burst out.

Panic filled his face, and he started to close the door, when Savannah heard a gun cock. "Open the door, Asahi," said Caruso from behind her. "And no quick moves, Sanchez." He yanked her gun from the back of her pants. "I was hoping it wouldn't come to this. Get inside."

The man he called Asahi backed up and held the door open as Caruso nudged Savannah inside with the butt of the gun. "Both of you in the center of the room and on the floor," he said.

Savannah raised her arms and turned around to face the detective. "Look Caruso, I don't know what is going on here, but I'm sure we can work something out."

"What's going on is that you stepped into something you shouldn't have. And it's Asahi's fault." He pointed the gun at the man and barked, "Get the packing tape."

The man scampered over to the table and returned with a roll of tape.

"Bind Sanchez's arms behind her back, then her feet. Make it tight."

As the man hurriedly restrained her, Savannah could feel his hands shaking. "You don't want to do this, Asahi," she said in a low voice.

Caruso glowered. "Keep talking, Sanchez, and I'll have him tape your mouth."

Once Asahi finished, Caruso ordered, "Now bind your own feet." Asahi did as he was told, fear in his eyes. Then the detective went over and bound Asahi's hands behind his back.

"You know what the consequences are for holding a federal officer?" said Sanchez. "You really want to torpedo your career?"

Caruso sniggered. "Career? The one that pays me pennies to risk my life. I'm going back for those orchids. Once the handoff to Asahi's father is complete, I'll send someone to untie you." Then he gave them a grim smile. "If the handoff doesn't go as planned, you'll both be meeting an unfortunate end."

"What about Becky Larson?" asked Savannah.

Caruso laughed. "That was just a ruse to get you and Larson out here with the orchids." Then he left, slamming the door behind him.

29

"There is an old saying that a man shows his true worth by what he values," said Nagaya to Brent. "I value my privacy, and yet here you are in my home."

Brent took a step toward the man when he suddenly felt a prick in the back of his neck. A burning sensation spread down his back as the floor began spinning underneath him. Brent fell to his knees and tried to crawl forward to stand, but the muscles in his arms and legs wouldn't support his body and he collapsed in a heap.

"What do you want me to do with him?" said another man's voice.

"Put him in the greenhouse while I figure out what to do about the agent and my son."

"Sanchez is mine," said the man. "That bitch is going to finally get what she deserves."

"Patience is not your virtue, Macintosh."

The man picked Brent up under the armpits, then dragged him down a hallway, opened a door, and dumped him inside. Brent tried to move, but couldn't. As he lay there, he began to feel a warm mist sprinkling his face. He smelled sphagnum moss and heard the faint whir of humidifiers.

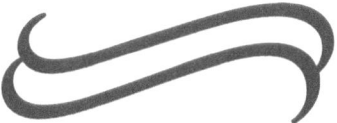

"You could have saved us all a lot of trouble if you had just come to me straight out and told me about your father and the orchids," said Savannah to Asahi.

"My father is a powerful man. I had to be cautious. Too many people have died for the orchids my father is so obsessed over. I tried to do the right thing."

"Your heart was in the right place, I'll give you that," said Savannah as she began scooting along the floor toward the table containing pieces of art. "Tell me you've got a box cutter or scissors in here somewhere."

For a time, Brent lay there immobile, his mind racing. He heard the misting system go on and off, and the fans hum. Then, finally, he felt tingling in his arms and legs and found he was able to move them. He put all his effort into pushing himself up, then leaned toward a nearby planter and slumped against it. He surveyed the scene. A climate-controlled greenhouse, complete with beds of colorful flowers. He spied lupines and daisies and something that caught his attention —foxglove, which contained digitalis. Doctors used it to stimulate hearts. It might counteract the effects of whatever they had given him.

After a few minutes, Brent managed to crawl the short distance to the planter containing foxglove. It took several tries for him to pull himself up enough to grab a leaf. Praying he didn't kill himself with this experiment, he put it into his mouth and ground it between his teeth the best he could. Before long, his heart began to race, and he felt adrenaline rush through his body. He attempted to stand and was able to stumble his way to the door where he turned the door handle gently. Unlocked. He peered outside. No one in sight. Feeling better by the moment, he left the room and headed down the hallway, soon coming to an open door. He crept in to find a home office lined with bookcases, and, in the center of the room, a giant mahogany desk with a painting on the wall behind it that made Brent gasp.

"There you are," said Nagaya, who came into the room behind him. "I didn't expect you to be moving around this soon." He looked up at the painting. "Night Lights. What a beautiful piece."

"Why would you steal that?" asked Brent as he looked around for a way to protect himself. He spotted an envelope opener on the edge of the desk.

"Technically, I didn't. I hired your old friend Jack Wallen to take it." He laughed then as if he'd made a joke.

"But why?"

"Your mother refused to sell it to me at her last show," he said. "I offered her more than a fair price, but she said the piece was spoken for. To be bequeathed to her son upon her death. Curiosity led me to find out more about you. Imagine my delight when I discovered that you oversaw an area home to my favorite plants, rare orchids."

Nagaya gazed up at the painting and said in a bemused tone, "I always intended to give everything to my only son.

All of this." He opened his arms wide. "But he isn't worthy. I just discovered that it was Asahi who told Agent Sanchez about my transgressions. My own son." The man frowned and shook his head. "You, on the other hand, your mother thought you were worthy of her finest work."

Brent grabbed the letter opener from the edge of the desk and pointed it at Nagaya. "Tell me where my sister is."

"My son's betrayal will bring great shame to my family name," said Nagaya, almost to himself. Then he took Brent by surprise by lunging at him and yanking the letter opener from his grasp. Brent backed up as the man raised the metal opener, then watched in horror as Nagaya plunged it into his own stomach. "I will not be dishonored," he choked the words out. His shirt quickly became soaked in blood, and he fell to his knees and onto his back.

Brent went to kneel beside him and checked his pulse. He must have hit an artery. The pulse was faint and then stopped. Brent stood and stared down at the man for a moment, then ran to the desk and began pulling open drawers. He needed to find keys to the Bentley he saw parked in the driveway.

"There are scissors up there on the table," said Asahi.

While lying on her back, Savannah reached her feet up onto the table and kicked. Several paintings fell to the floor, then the scissors clattered onto the concrete. She writhed her way toward them, then turned herself around and picked them up with her fingers. Once she managed to open them, she began sawing at the tape on her wrists. As she worked, she cut herself several times and felt the blood slick against her fingers, but she kept working at it. She was almost free when the door opened, letting in the midday sun and temporarily blinding her.

A voice said, "I wouldn't bother, Sanchez." He slammed the door and came to tower over Savannah, who looked up into the cold, gray eyes of William Macintosh.

"You could have started a whole new life under another identity," she said. "But you came back. Why?"

Macintosh knelt next to Savannah; his breath smelled like tobacco. "To finish what I started. You should have died that night along with your husband. Thanks to you, I lost everything."

Savannah studied his face. "Revenge is a weak man's reason for living."

Macintosh's eyes filled with rage at her words. He stood and pulled a lighter out of his pocket. "Thanks to the dry brush out here, all the loose ends will soon be ashes."

He stalked to the table and took an armful of paintings and left with them, returning twice more until they were all gone. Then he dragged Savannah to the table and taped her wrists around one of the legs. Turning to Asahi, he announced, "You're coming with me to offload the paintings. But first, we're going to have a convincing talk with Larson about what happened to those orchids." He slit through the tape on Asahi's legs with the scissors and yanked him to his feet, then marched him out and slammed the door.

After a few minutes, Savannah heard a car start up and pull away. Then she smelled smoke. Every fiber in her body sprang into high alert.

30

Brent found a Calabasas address in the Bentley's GPS system and sped that way. He prayed that Macintosh had gotten waylaid looking for the orchids at the LAPD and hadn't gotten to Savannah yet. He pushed the car to the limit as he exited the freeway offramp. Anxiety thrummed in his chest when he saw a heavy plume of gray smoke in the distance. As he drove, a car approached, going in the opposite direction. When it passed in a blur, Brent thought he saw two men.

After several long, grueling minutes, Brent arrived at the property and gunned the engine down the driveway. Braking in front of the building, he saw it was engulfed in flames. He ran to the front door to find it ajar and kicked it all the way open, then pulled his shirt up over his mouth and entered, scanning the room for signs of Savannah and his sister. Through the increasing smoke, he spied someone on the floor across the room. Bending as low as possible, he rushed over to find Savannah slumped over. He tried to pick her up, but she had been bound to the table with tape. Looking around as the smoked burned his eyes and choked him, he saw a pair of scissors on the floor and cut her free. Then he picked Savannah up and ran, just as an ablaze ceiling beam fell to the side of them. Putting everything he had into the final sprint, he rushed out of the building and kept going until he reached the side of the road, where he stopped and laid Savannah down in the dry brush.

"Savannah," he cried, checking her pulse. It was weak, and she didn't appear to be breathing. He tipped her head back and began giving her mouth to mouth. Just when he thought he might have lost her, Savannah began gasping for air and opened her beautiful green eyes.

"Thank God," he said, helping her to sit up as she began to cough. "Was Becky with you?" His heart skipped wildly as he glanced back to see the house now completely covered in flames.

"Your sister...," said Savannah, her voice raspy. She tried to swallow. "Your sister is okay."

Relief flowing through him, Brent took the tape from around her wrists, which was covered in blood, and freed her feet. She sat hunched over on the ground next to him. "Can you stand?" he asked. "The fire is spreading. We need to start moving."

"How'd you get here?" she asked as he helped her up.

"I took Nagaya's car, but it's too close to the house now to access."

"Nagaya?" she said as fire trucks sounded nearby.

"I went to his house to find Becky. Do you have any idea," the words choked from his mouth, "where she is?"

"They never took her. It was a trick to get us here with the orchids."

Two fire trucks hurried toward them and onto the property. Then came a police car, followed by an ambulance.

An officer got out of the squad car and walked toward them. Before he could speak, Savannah said, "I'm Agent Sanchez with the FBI. You can call our headquarters in DC and ask to speak to Supervisor Sully to verify my credentials."

The officer nodded, then got on the phone. After he hung up, he said, "Can you tell me what occurred here?"

"As soon as I make a call."

Cherie answered before the phone even rang. "Boss, I've been trying to get ahold of you. The team landed an hour ago. What's going on?"

"Macintosh is on the move, and he's got a hostage, an Asahi Nagaya. They've got some stolen paintings they're going to fence, then Macintosh will likely be in the wind again." After Savannah finished giving Cherie the details, she handed the officer his phone, and began coughing hard.

"I think it'd be a good idea if you both get examined," said the officer. He gestured to a paramedic standing nearby, who walked them to the ambulance.

After checking both of their vitals and lungs, the paramedic said to Brent, "You're okay, but Agent Sanchez, you need to go to the hospital for oxygen therapy. I'm going to start you on some now."

Savannah's first instinct was to protest, but Brent took her arm and urged, "You were unconscious and not breathing when I found you." Then he said to the paramedic, "I want to go with her."

The man nodded as he got Savannah settled on a gurney. Brent took her hand as they headed away from the fire, sirens wailing behind them.

An hour later, the doctor had talked Savannah into spending the night on oxygen. The nurse wheeled a cot in for Brent and went to get Savannah dinner. When she got a call, he took a moment to walk out into the hallway and call Becky. She answered on the first ring.

"Where have you been?" she said. "I was about to call in the National Guard!"

"It's so good to hear your voice," said Brent, tears burning at the back of his eyes. He leaned against the hospital wall and smiled. "I'm sorry. I was off the grid."

"You sound funny. You okay?"

Brent glanced into the room at Savannah, who had taken out the oxygen tubing and was animatedly talking on her phone.

"More than okay."

"Were you camping by yourself again?" his sister asked. "Seriously, big brother, you need to get a real life."

"I haven't been by myself. I met this beautiful FBI agent. Then I got shot, and I just rescued her from a fire. Is that exciting enough for you?"

Becky laughed the high-pitched trill that couldn't help but make Brent chuckle. "Very funny. Okay, point taken. Hey, I finished that commercial, and I've got a little break. I was thinking I could come visit you next week."

Brent moved out of the way as a nurse brought a tray of food into Savannah's room. "How about if I come to you?"

"To LA? Sure. When?"

"How about tomorrow?"

"What?"

"I'm already in LA. I want you to meet someone."

"OMG! You met someone? Like really met someone?" Becky squealed. "I can't wait! Is she nice? Of course, she's nice."

Brent laughed. "I'll see you tomorrow." He went back into the hospital room to find Savannah eating her dinner.

"Either this isn't half bad, or I'm just desperate for food. You want some?" she asked.

Brent shook his head. "Was that your team on the phone?"

"Yes. They nabbed Macintosh trying to sell the paintings, and they caught Caruso getting on a flight to the Cayman Islands. Turns out Caruso is the one who killed that woman you found in the marsh. She was an environmental activist and was going to blow the whistle. The Poolesville police picked up Jack Wallen for stealing your painting, among other offenses." She stopped and took a drink of water.

"Did they retrieve the orchids?" asked Brent.

"Yes, they're safe and sound. And they got your painting from Nagaya's house. Nagaya Jr. is in trouble, but they're going to consider that he tried to stop things by coming to me. They also got the fire under control before it turned into a wildfire. You get ahold of your sister?"

"I did," said Brent. "If okay with you, I'd like to go see her tomorrow."

Savannah waved her fork in the air. "Whatever you want. The case is officially over."

Brent felt an empty feeling fill his chest at Savannah's words. Had he read this all wrong? Afraid that his face might betray him, he said suddenly, "I'm going to the cafeteria to get a bite."

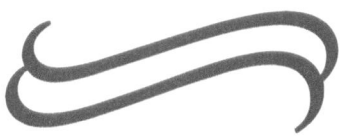

Savannah watched Brent leave and felt angry at herself. He'd risked his life for her, and all she could do was talk official business. Why couldn't she tell him how she felt? That she really cared for him, and wanted to be with him? She pushed the meal away and kept her eyes on the door, anxious as she waited for Brent to return. When he did, she was going to tell him how she felt. But time ticked by, and no Brent. Finally, Savannah closed her eyes to rest.

When Brent returned from the cafeteria, he found Savannah asleep. He got comfortable in the cot and fastened his eyes on her, listening to the soft, even way she sounded as she slept. This would all be over tomorrow when the doctor released her, but for now he would enjoy being near Savannah.

In the middle of the night, Brent was awoken by Savannah moaning. He sat up in the cot and leaned close. Was she dreaming? He was about to lie back down when she cried out his name. He took her hand. "I'm here."

Her eyes fluttered open, and she focused on him. Then she reached out and wrapped the fingers of one hand around his wrist. "Brent," she murmured, "there's something I need to tell you."

"It can wait until morning," he said. "Try to rest."

"No," she said, her tone urgent. She took off the oxygen tubing.

"What is it?" He helped prop pillows behind her head.

"I wanted to thank you for saving my life."

"You don't need to thank me," he said, and gave a low laugh.

"And something else." She turned to face him more fully. "There's no easy way to say this." She began to cough.

Brent's heart sank at her words, afraid of what she was about to say. He reached for a cup of water on the bedside table and handed it to her. She took several swallows.

"Tell me," he said.

"It's just that.... I don't know if I have the right words to say what I'm feeling." She pressed her lips together and tried again. "You mean so much to me, and, well, I'm willing, that is, if you think…"

Brent stared at Savannah when he realized what she was trying to say.

"Darn it," she said, finally. "I think, okay, I know. I'm falling in love with you."

He took a deep breath and smiled, his eyes never leaving her face.

"You can say something now," she said, the sheet balled in one fist.

Brent leaned over and kissed Savannah gently on the lips, then said, "I've already fallen in love with you. And I definitely don't want this to end."

EPILOGUE

Savannah's and Brent's stories are complete, but Cherie Tomlinson's is just beginning....

Cherie Tomlinson set her carry-on bag next to her at the airport café. Finally, the vacation to Puerto Vallarta she'd been dreaming about for months. She smiled when the waitress approached.

"What can I get for you, honey?"

Even though she wasn't usually a drinker, Cherie decided to celebrate. "A Mai Tai," she said, then added, "with an extra splash of triple sec."

"You got it," said the waitress, turning to take the next table's order.

Cherie looked over to see an incredibly handsome man. He had close-cropped black hair and wore the sexy stubble of someone who hadn't shaved for a couple of days. When he finished ordering, he glanced at Cherie, who was still staring.

"Are you coming or going?" the man asked.

"Are you talking to me?" Cherie asked.

He laughed. "Yes."

Cherie pulled a napkin from the dispenser on the table and replied, "Going. Puerto Vallarta."

"It just so happens that I'm also going to Puerto Vallarta," he said as the waitress put Cherie's drink in front of her, then handed the mystery man a beer.

"May I?" he asked, gesturing with his head at the other seat at her table.

Cherie nodded awkwardly, then managed to reply, "Of course."

The man stood up and came toward her. He was muscular, his biceps and pecs apparent through his tight-fitting shirt. He sat down and asked, "Are you from the DC area?"

"I am," she said, taking a drink of the Mai Tai, hoping the alcohol would ease the overly excited thrumming of her heart. "Are you from here?"

He took a long pull of his beer and replied, "Just passing through." He stuck out his hand. "I'm Justin."

Cherie took his hand, warm and firm, and they shook. "Cherie."

"So, what kind of work do you do?" he asked her.

"I work in a government job." Her boss had taught her it was best not to let people know she was FBI.

"Sounds mysterious," he said, smiling.

"What about you?"

"I'm a painter."

"Oh, as in artist?" asked Cherie.

He laughed. "No, buildings and such."

Just then, a voice came over the intercom, announcing it was time to board their flight. Cherie reached for her bag.

Justin stood. "After you."

As they exited the café and headed across the corridor for their gate, a military policeman walked by, the letters MP emblazoned on his shirt. Cherie stopped as he passed, curious as to what could be going on. Then before she knew what was happening, Justin clasped his arm around her waist and pulled her close. Startled, she looked up to see he had pulled a baseball cap low over his face.

"Keep walking slowly to the gate," he said in a low voice. "We're getting on the flight together."

Read Cherie's story in *Discovered Suspicion*.

A NOTE FOR YOU

Dear Reading Gem,

Thanks for spending time with me, Savannah and Brent! While each of the books in the Discovered Truth Series can be read as a standalone, it's fun to experience the progression and get to know the characters. The series progresses as minor characters introduced in each book become main characters in subsequent books. It's exciting to see what they'll do next!

The Discovered Truth series features complex, gutsy women and equally complicated, charismatic men who find themselves immersed in dangerous and intriguing modern-day challenges, such as human trafficking, drug smuggling, organ theft, national security threats, and identity theft. When the heroine and hero meet, worlds collide and sparks fly, kindling unforgettable romance and intrigue.

Thanks again and talk soon!

STAY ENLIGHTENED

Dear Reading Gem, thanks for reading! Let's stay in touch.

Join my weekly newsletter Julie's Reading Gems here. You get a free prequel novella to the series for signing up. There are also weekly giveaways and contests to win free books in the series.

You can also find me on my website at https://www.juliebawdendavis.com/fiction, email me at Julie@JulieBawdenDavis.com, and follow me on Amazon.

Escape to Unforgettable Romance and Intrigue...

YOUR OPINION MATTERS

If you liked this book, please leave a review on Amazon, GoodReads, BookBub, or all three. If you don't wish to leave a review or don't have time, please leave a rating. Every star helps!

BOOKS IN THE DISCOVERED TRUTH SERIES

Discovered Beginnings:
(FREE at https://www.juliebawdendavis.com/fiction)
Discovered Secrets
Discovered Memories
Discovered Indiscretions
Discovered Liaisons
Discovered Betrayal
Discovered Denial
Discovered Distractions
Discovered Deception
Discovered Lies
Discovered Vengeance
Discovered Redemption
Discovered Obsession
Discovered Transgressions
Discovered Suspicion
Discovered Escape
Discovered Promises
Discovered Cover-up

BOOKS IN THE DISCOVERED TRUTH SERIES

Box Sets

The Discovered Truth Series Box Set Books 1-4
The Discovered Truth Series Box Set Books 5-8
The Discovered Truth Series Box Set Books 9-12
The Discovered Truth Series Box Set Books 13-16

·

www.ingramcontent.com/pod-product-compliance
Lightning Source LLC
Chambersburg PA
CBHW022127170626
46808CB00002B/875